"Lady Sinom?"

Mehga touched the old woman's shoulder gently. She might be a political enemy, but her person certainly deserved respect. "Sinom, I must go now—"

"You're not going anywhere!" The wheelchair spun around. Mehga's eyes opened wide as the color vanished from her face. Fully exposed to the hideous countenance, she wavered, then dropped to her knees.

"You wanted the truth? Well, here it is. Come inside us now, Mehga dear. Let us show you what we really are!"

Mike Conner
Groupmind

BERKLEY BOOKS, NEW YORK

GROUPMIND

A Berkley Book / published by arrangement with
the author

PRINTING HISTORY
Berkley edition / October 1984

ISBN: 0-425-07191-X

This Is for RAC
Dear Old Dad.

Book One

MINDCOUP

CHAPTER 1

The thing called a Xein was roughly the size of a crab, had twelve pincerlike claws, and it could fly by spinning like a buzz saw when it wanted to. Presently it stood still, gripping the far anchor post of a rope footbridge and blinking accusingly at its hesitant master on the other side.

"I'm coming, Janoo." First Speaker Rowen laughed, but unconvincingly. The ravine before him—a chasm cutting all the way through the terrace—might as well have been the whole canyon, because the fear that gripped him at the thought of crossing the bridge was the same. Ridiculous as it seemed, the leader of a people whose entire population was housed in a sixty-three-mile-deep crack in the surface of an otherwise inhospitable planet was afraid of heights.

Nervously he glanced upslope, where Tyron's crew was busy excavating a trench lined on either side with aboriginal stone carvings. Rowen needed to speak with the archaeologist about his findings, and he knew the old man was waiting for him in the shack that overlooked the dig. Short of flying like Janoo, there was no other convenient way to cross. Using a floater was forbidden, for fear that the engine vibration might crumble

3

the fragile sandstone inside the trench. So there was no choice, really. Rowen licked his lips and stepped out onto the springy plank deck of the bridge. He pulled himself ahead with his arms, and only when his feet stumbled against worn stone did he realize his passage was completed—and that his eyes had been tightly closed.

"Too proud to ask for help?" The archaeologist Tyron stood on top of a pile of unsorted till and peered down like an eagle surveying its territory. He was a tall, proud man, and though he was more than three hundred years old, he still possessed a barrel chest and the powerful arms of someone a quarter that age. He frowned when Janoo buzzed the top of his head, but he didn't duck.

"You put that bridge there on purpose, I'll swear!" Rowen's heartbeat was slowing to normal.

"Of course I did! Only thing worse than government fools tripping all over is this thing!" Tyron reached into his pocket for a fig, which he threw far upslope. Janoo caught it on the fly and settled onto the turf to eat.

"Still, I suppose you're here. Come in!"

Rowen followed him along the trench. Where the ancient slabs had been cleaned of detritus he could make out a procession of carved figures. The bodies were stiff but humanoid enough; the faces were covered with reptilian masks. Rowen stared in fascination at the last of the figures until he realized that Tyron was impatiently holding the shack door open for him.

"Some tea?" Tyron asked as they went inside.

"No, thank you." Rowen stepped around a pile of books. The interior of the shack was nothing but piles —of dishes, tapes, notebooks, clothing. Somehow, the old man produced a pot and put some water to boil on his camp stove.

"Well, First Speaker. To what do I owe this great honor!" Rowen detected a twinkle in the fierce eyes, but that did not keep him from feeling like a boy caught breaking a window. Tyron had always made him feel that way, and probably always would. He cleared his throat.

"I've come to ask whether you've made any progress deciphering these carvings."

"Progress? Since when does archaeology interest you?"

"Like anyone, I need outside interests to remain fresh. And rumors eventually filter down to Conteirre City."

"Rumors!" Tyron spat through an open window. Across the excavation site and the expanse of the terrace dropping gradually toward the hazy maw of the canyon were the slender, jewel-like towers of the capital, which caught the last of the afternoon light reflected into the canyon by the great Dragonshack mirror array on the surface. "Politically useful rumors, I suppose. You wouldn't be thinking of Mother Sinom and her Committee, would you?"

Rowen waved his hand. "A cult. Nothing but a troublesome cult."

"You're quick to dismiss it, Speaker? But the practice of linking minds through her continues to gain popularity. The religious mumbo jumbo, that's nothing. But the economic and political consequences if Sinom's movement gains strength? Quite serious indeed!"

"I'm glad to hear you have outside interests of your own, Tyron."

The old man laughed. "Come with me, Speaker. I want to show you something."

They went through the back of the shack and down a temporary stairway to a further excavation of the trench. Tyron turned on some spotlights.

"Here. We've uncovered a sequence of petroglyphs that we call the flaming circle. Repeated all along the arcade. First a procession in the reptile masks. Then a linking together around this."

Rowen bent close to peer at the carvings. "A serpent?"

"Consuming its own tail. Here, notice how in the

next sequence the details are less distinct. And here, in the last, the individuals in the circle have faded away completely."

"They seem afraid," Rowen said.

"What makes you say that?"

"Their posture. The extended arms. And something else . . . I get the feeling that whoever carved these was horrified by the story he was trying to tell."

Tyron smiled fiercely. "You may be in the wrong profession, Speaker! You haven't noticed something obvious, though."

"What's that?"

"The glyphs lead here." Tyron walked to a roped-off section of the trench. Where the cut into the terrace had been halted stood a pair of gleaming, lozenge-shaped stones, each as tall as a man.

"Your rumor, Speaker. One of my assistants put his hands on these stones when they were first uncovered. The results were interesting. He claimed he heard voices —pleas, cries for help. That was followed by a sensation of intense cold. We literally had to pry him off, and even then, he lost an arm. Frostbite."

Rowen looked at the stones, which seemed to absorb the output from the floodlights. He rubbed his hands together.

"What's your opinion, Tyron?"

"My opinion." He shook his head. "It's a pity you can't interview the man. But he's quite mad. Quite mad. If you want to know what I think, look at the stones. Aboriginals joining together, then fading away until nothing is left but these two stones. I can't explain it, Rowen. In my opinion, it's a warning."

"Against?"

"I won't presume to say. Those are the constraints of the scientist. You, however, have no such constraints. A warning against group consciousness, Rowen? If that is what you seek, it's here. An interview with a man who's gone mad? That too could be quite useful." His eyes narrowed. "Especially if you fear Sinom more than you say."

Rowen's smile was faint. "I'm due in Weiring soon. Inspecting the harbor facilities. I shall consider what you have shown me, Tyron. Thank you."

"As long as you're at it, consider this too: Think twice about resigning your office, Speaker. These are interesting times. Too interesting!" He walked past Rowen and disappeared into his shack. For a moment, the First Speaker of the Citizenry of Conteirre was too stunned to follow along.

Tyron customarily took a nap late each afternoon to refresh himself before the work of the evening. He was dozing in his favorite chair when a pair of cowled men entered the shack. One of them kicked at Tyron's feet.

"Wake up, old man!"

The words were unnecessary, for Tyron had heard them coming. Although the light was dim, he knew who they were. Their starburst cowl clasps were all he needed to see.

"Everyone's interested in poor old Tyron these days."

"On your feet, if you value your life!"

"*You* value it more. Fancy carrying me to your mistress?"

One of the visitors answered him with a blow. Tyron tasted blood and knew he was to be made an example of. A convert for Sinom's Committee. The Citizenry would not know, of course, that his conversion had been forced. Abruptly he decided what to do and stood.

"Save your strength," he snapped. "I won't resist." Tyron watched them closely, and when they relaxed—it was only slightly—he wheeled and charged out the rear of the shack. The spotlights had been extinguished when Rowan had left, and Tyron had the advantage of knowing the ground. He was at the end of the trench before his pursuit had even stumbled down the stairs.

"Want me, old woman? See if you can take me!"

He put his hands on the stones. His scream was loud, but he did not hear it, and by the time the cowled men pulled him away it had faded to a mere rattle in his throat. One of the men put his hand to the side of his head.

"Yes, my lady. We'll take him there."

Slowly they dragged him out of the trench and into a waiting floater.

CHAPTER 2

The adopted planet of the Citizenry of Conteirre was a nearly airless, silica-rich world surfaced with immense sand plains bounded by humpbacked mountain ranges and deep canyons. These were a product of crustal shrinkage aeons ago, and a few extended nearly from pole to pole. During the summer months, when the planet's elliptical orbit brought it close to its yellow sun, sandstorms made the dunes march. Winter brought quiescence and a little carbon dioxide snow.

It was very different from the Citizenry's first home. That had been a water world, thickly forested, with fjords reaching into warm, life-giving oceans. There, on the verge of land and water, a civilization had been born that grew and matured. And there it would have stayed if the sun had not failed.

When that happened, some Citizens felt that Conteirre should suffer fate with dignity and allow itself to perish. The stronger party, lead by Rowen's father, Raeger, advocated an exodus, and in the end, the Citizenry opted for survival. It was Lady Sinom, leader of the Committee of Two Hundred and old even then, who had helped to locate the abandoned canyon world. And it was Raeger, and then Rowen, who had stripped the homeworld bare and took everything it had to give in order to save those who wanted to preserve their own lives, and the life of the Citizenry.

And now the Citizenry lived on forty-three terraces staggered on the walls of a canyon twenty miles across and sixty-three deep, a canyon groomed to resemble as much as possible the cindered incinerated homeland. Waterfalls driven by the updrafts into rainbow curtains nourished the rich farmlands of the broad middle terraces, while farther below, new fjords had been sculpted into the great bottom reservoir, Lake Alissia. Clouds born in the sea climbed the terraces past hanging gardens, and even into regions of ice and snow.

On every level there were cities. Weiring, with its fleets of trawlers seining the waters stocked by the departed aborigines: Meems, nestled against the tremendous penstocks that circulated hydraulic fluid from the collector grid outside the mouth of the canyon. And the jewel, Conteirre City, transported brick by brick from the homeworld, now a floating crown to the achievements of her Citizens. It symbolized hope for the future, hope that the adopted planet could become what the homeworld had been.

Inside the canyon, one could believe that hope had already been achieved. Outside existed stark proof of the work that lay ahead. Barren, brown, lifeless, the outside was a place few Citizens could remain in for very long without suffering a profound sense of loss. Accordingly, there were only a few scattered scientific and industrial outposts on the surface, whose personnel was rotated quickly back into the moist womb of the Citizenry.

There was one permanent resident, however.

Close by the mechanisms that turned the Dragonsback mirror array was a pressure dome set inside a manmade crater. Drifting sand covered part of it in the lee of the prevailing westerlies, but plows kept the well-used roadway to the dome airlocks clear at all times. The dome was the home of Lady Sinom, and headquarters for her Committee of Two Hundred.

The compound was as stark as the surface of Conteirre. Most of the buildings were converted construction trailers used by Sinom's increasing numbers of visitors. These were arranged around a theater consisting of a slab stage and glass-stump seats. Next to it lay the only green patch on the whole planet: Sinom's garden. Often, visitors would see her, a hunched figure in a wheelchair, dressed always in dazzling white, moving from row to row thinning root crops, or gathering glistening purple eggplants.

It was not permitted for any pilgrim, or any of the Committee staff who might have business in the compound, to enter this garden without the direct permission of the one who tended it. It was the only rule Sinom had ever imposed here, and not even Gaelen, the strapping Deputy Speaker of the Diet of Citizens, had leave to violate the edict.

Presently Gaelen stood at the fence, fidgeting. He cleared his throat several times. Finally—though loath to do so—he violated the silence.

"Mother Sinom?"

"What is it, Gaelen?" As always, her voice surprised him. Nobody knew how old she really was. But her voice was as light and clear as that of a girl.

"May I have a word with you."

"Come. I'm nearly finished."

Gaelen took a deep breath and entered the sacrosanct ground. Sinom turned her chair suddenly to face him; Gaelen stopped short. Fortunately, Sinom wore a heavy veil today. Gaelen was relieved, for, although he had been her protégé for more than a dozen years, he had never seen her face, nor did he want to. Sinom's good eye, brown and impassive, was all he could see, all he ever wanted to see. As always when speaking to her, Gaelen came directly to the point.

"Your instructions have been carried out. Tyron's installed in a suspension cell for all to see."

"A pity I couldn't see him first, Gaelen."

"There were difficulties. He's no longer in his right mind."

"I know all about it!" The voice tightened—all it took to convey Sinom's considerable displeasure. "The thing was done clumsily. Your men ought at least to have locked that door. He's lost to me now."

"Yes." Gaelen brightened. "But I have prevailed upon Secretary Mehga to accompany me here. It was difficult. She's very nervous about the general assembly Rowen's called for tomorrow." Gaelen hesitated. "Have you . . . *seen* what he intends to do?"

"You know better than to ask me that."

"I only meant that knowing Rowen's plan would make his wife easier to handle now."

Sinom was amused. "Shall I have you behind the arras to prompt me, Gaelen?"

"Of course not. But I worked long and hard to get her this far."

"You must learn to have more confidence in your efforts! Which cabin is she in?"

"Six. I'll escort her to your house."

"No. I shall go to her."

Gaelen frowned. "Let me prepare her then."

"You'll attend to your business." Again the voice seemed unperturbed, but when Sinom's wheelchair began to move, Gaelen scrambled back. He had been dismissed. And he had no desire to remain in Sinom's garden alone.

The Secretary of the Diet of Citizens had made up her mind to leave the Committee compound. Mehga had been restless ever since the Deputy Speaker had taken her to this trailer. Now, cursing herself for having allowed Gaelen to sway her with glib talk, she started to pull from her head the cowl that all visitors to the Committee wore.

I'm a fool, she thought. These people were her political enemies, and she was wasting her time when she should be on her way down to Weiring to meet her husband.

The cabin door opened just as Mehga got the cowl off. A veiled woman all in white pulled her wheelchair effortlessly up the ramp. Mehga clumsily tried to slip the cowl back on, only to be interrupted by Sinom's surprisingly gentle laughter.

"That isn't necessary, Madame Secretary. You are very welcome here as you are."

Mehga smiled and put the garment onto the cot. Hoping she didn't sound as startled as she felt, she said, "It's an honor to finally meet Conteirre's oldest Citizen."

"I shall have to consider that a compliment, won't I? Please sit down. I'm afraid there's not much chance of my standing."

Disarmed, Mehga complied.

"There now! Let me get a look at you." Sinom's brown eye was calm and impassive. At length, the Lady said, "The pictures I've seen don't do you justice. A most youthful eighty-seven."

"Thank you." Mehga found herself staring at Sinom's veil.

"You're nervous. Everyone's always nervous around me! Even Gaelen." She chuckled. "But I suppose it can't be helped. I'm not a pretty sight." Sinom reached for the starburst clasp that held the cloth at her cheek. "Would you like to see? Imagination can be an evil conjuror."

"Please don't—I mean, perhaps when we know each other better."

Abruptly, Sinom wheeled around to the tiny cooler chest beside the cot. She got out a pair of water bottles, opened both, and handed one to the Secretary.

"You're right, of course. And I admit I do make a test of my face at times. There's no need for that now. You're not a silly Midlands farmgirl!"

Mehga watched with fascination as the old woman pushed the bottle underneath the veil, lifting it slightly as she tilted her head to drink. The skin of her neck was loose and very dark, with a shiny talus of scar tissue reaching toward her hidden chin. For a moment, Mehga feared the cloth might drop. She fully intended to flee if it did.

"May we talk about your fear, Madame Secretary? Why is it you fear me so much?"

"I apologize if I give you that impression, Lady. How could I fear you? We've only just met."

"This room reeks with fear! Your fear of me makes my own skin crawl, precisely as if you were a mirror. Don't blush so! I'm not interested in humiliating you, only in getting the usual evasions out of the way. You fear me. The question is, why?"

Inwardly, Mehga was dismayed at the course the interview had taken. She'd expected a diplomatic exchange of pleasantries, perhaps a tour of the compound, all carefully controlled, the questions all her own. She took a breath.

"Very well, Lady, since you seem to value frank talk, I'll tell you. You—and your Committee—are a political threat whose power is an unknown quantity. You seem to have created a movement whose influence grows each day. I came because I want to know that enemy. Someday I will be called to take the Speaker's chair. I'm telling you now that I consider your Committee as great a threat to the Citizenry as the nova which forced us to take refuge here."

"That is not your husband's opinion."

"Rowen and I disagree on many points."

"But you are in full accord philosophically. Like him, you see the development of this planet as the first order of business."

"We want to make Conteirre more comfortable, yes."

"And then?"

"We move on. Colonize other worlds, contact other races sympathetic to our form of life."

"Continue to work and strive until the galaxy's ours, eh? Then what? A universe there for the taking?"

Mehga smiled, relaxing slightly. "Actually, I'm more concerned with the silt reclamation project at Northend at the moment."

The tires of Sinom's chair squeaked on the metal floor as she came close. "You know, of course, that it's never been possible to build a bridge to paradise."

"We should try, all the same."

"Ah, Rowen has taught you well—as his father and
Tyron taught him. The materialist lives in blissful ignor-
ance. But I haven't had that luxury, Madame Secretary.
Unlike you, I know the value of a body when it won't
stand straight, when other people require a shot of mor-
phia to look at it! I've been forced—privileged—to go
beyond my body, to touch a deeper, more glorious life.
And if others wish to join me, that is their right. More
than their right! It is their duty! I have been considerate
of political obstacles for many years. I have chosen to
ignore the ingratitude of the Speaker, who has forgotten
who it was who led the Citizenry to this refuge. But that
time is over, Madame Secretary! The Citizenry is ready
now to embrace the concept of group consciousness.
When it has, it will then be time to build the apparatus,
the economic and physical structure to support it."

Mehga stood. Here was talk she understood, talk she
could deal with. "Lady, I hear this sort of thing every
session of the Diet. Your Committee will continue to re-
tain the same rights and privileges as all other religions.
Nothing more, nothing less. But as long as I have anything to say about it, the government will never promote
or build or support suspension facilities such as you
have constructed outside Conteirre City. I will be seeking an injunction to prevent the use of such cells within
the canyon. And I will win. Our people are builders,
Lady, not dreamers."

Mehga saw then that Sinom's eye had closed, that the
old woman seemed to have fallen asleep. Was this the
mighty Sinom? She felt disappointment, but elation
too, for she understood now the key to defeating the
Committee. Strip the veil of mystery away. Show the
people what Sinom was, and exactly what she offered:
empty years of wasting away inside a suspension cell.
Perhaps Rowen was right. Perhaps the threat was not so
serious as she'd feared.

"Lady Sinom?" Mehga touched the old woman's
shoulder gently. She might be a political enemy, but her

person certainly deserved respect. "Sinom, I must go now."

"You're not going anywhere!" The wheelchair spun around. Mehga's eyes opened wide as the color vanished from her face. She wavered, then dropped to her knees. Sinom held her veil in her fist.

"You wanted the truth? Well, here it is. Come inside us now, Mehga dear. Let us show you what we are."

The old woman reached out and took Mehga's head in her soft, wrinkled hands.

CHAPTER 3

Rowen leaned against the bow rail of the fishing trawler as it dished through Lake Alissia's wind-whipped swells on the return journey to Weiring harbor. Parry, who was Weiring Harbormaster, stood close and yelled his tour narration against the crash of the swells and the roaring engines below decks, but the First Speaker caught little of his host's speech. He was thinking of Tyron and his own decision to retire. Uncanny, how the old man had got beyond the words to the truth. Uncanny, but not completely unexpected.

"Storm's building, Harbormaster!" Rowen pointed to the squall line south of Weiring's new jetty. By now night had already fallen on the upper terraces, but that by no means sentenced the broad reservoir on the canyon floor to darkness. The walls and exposed structures of this part of Conteirre fluoresced long after sunset, and the pale, diffuse glow lent Lake Alissia's whitecaps an ectoplasmic quality. It was as if the hands of dead men and women had breached the shimmery green surface of the lake, gesturing, imploring, grabbing if they could. The trawler continued to plow through, shattering them to mist that soaked through Rowen's jacket and hair. He could see squall lines building on both sides of the lake, feeding on the moist updrafts off the

17

warm water. Where this current touched cold dry air falling from the darkened heights there were eddies and multiple flashes of lightning. The clouds were ghostly too: bloated giants challenging the impassive overhang of terraces one and two. Weiring would get wet tonight.

Now, as the pilot cut throttle to enter the breakwater, Rowen was again able to hear his host clearly. "We're doing our best with what we have down here. I've made a written report for you to look at later, when you get the chance."

Later. How he wished he could tell this man there would be no later for First Speaker Rowen. Parry thinks I don't care what sort of job he's done. Or worse, that I suspect him of lining his pockets. He clapped the harbormaster on the back. "Thank you. I appreciate your arranging a tour on such short notice." Rowen winked. "I'll keep it a secret, though. We don't want to bring too many visitors down from the City. Hey! Here comes the fleet."

Parry's trawler whistled its salute as a good three dozen boats—some glass, some plastic, and one or two wooden relicts—steamed by on their way to an evening's catch of marl and skate. Rowen had seen such scenes many times as a boy—among the fjords of the homeworld. It was said that a person could dream slow dreams while locked inside a funeral block. If this were true, Rowen knew he would return to the homeworld again when the day came for him to surrender active life. Until that day, however, it was fine to see Citizens engaged in the old trades.

"I wish I might have come on a fair night, Parry. It would be glorious to see all the boats leaving the harbor at once."

But Rowen's remark only seemed to increase the Harbormaster's discomfort. For a moment Rowen had the impression that Parry wanted to explain something to him. But he said nothing, and when the trawler moved into its berth he busied himself with the mooring lines. Rowen hopped onto the dock and performed a few deep knee bends to get his land legs back.

"You're wet, sir! Come to my house and I'll lend you a sweater. And a hot brandy if you'll take it."

"Some other time, Harbormaster. I have a speech to prepare, and need some time alone. There's a grove not far from the outskirts of Weiring where I go when I'm having trouble composing my thoughts."

"It does me good to know you have such troubles too, Speaker." Parry smiled. Rowen opened the side of the floater he'd parked near the quay. Then he noticed several young men and women who lay on a spit of sand a little off from the harbor.

"Isn't that your son over there? You should have asked him to come with us. I haven't seen him since he was a little boy." Rowen halted. The Harbormaster was perpetually worried, but now he looked close to tears.

"I'd hoped you wouldn't see. You, of all people!"

Another look and Rowen understood. The youths lay still, cradled in shallow trenches dug into the fine wet sand. Even though the rising tide now covered their legs and feet, no one had moved, or even seemed aware of the danger. They might have been asleep, or dead.

Mindlinked. Those who practiced the techniques taught by the Committee typically lost all awareness of their surroundings, surrendering themselves totally to Sinom's guidance and control. As part of the group consciousness, their personal safety and integrity meant nothing.

Fury rose in him, shockingly intense.

These people were thrill seekers, playing with forces they couldn't possibly understand, forces Citizens had never been meant to understand. His first reaction was to summon the Weiring Prefect and have the reckless youngsters committed for seventy-two hours of psychiatric observation and Healing. Such an action was well within the scope of his powers, and this would not be the first time he had used them in that way.

But Parry's humiliation—and Rowen had to admit it, Parry's fear—dissuaded him. "Come on," he ordered, heading toward the beach. Parry followed, breathlessly trying to explain.

"We've done all we can to stop him, but it's like a drug! All his friends—all the young people in Weiring—have tried it. I tell him it's wrong, but there's nothing I can say that he'll listen to."

Rowen jumped from the curb. "Look at this. The water could cover their faces and they'd never even know." Parry's son was one of the linkers down close to the water; Rowen grabbed the youth's arm and pulled him to a sitting position. The muscles of his body were flaccid, his breathing shallow and slow. And though Arden's eyes were open, the pupils were almost completely dilated. Rowen shook him roughly.

"Arden! Arden, wake up!"

Arden blinked several times, frowning, but the expression didn't take. Rowen slapped him.

"Speaker Rowen!"

"You want him back, don't you? Help with some of the others, quickly!" Raindrops had started driving pockmarks into the moist sand as Rowen hit the boy once more. Suddenly Arden came to with a snarl, swinging wildly with both hands and striking Rowen's face. Rowen rolled back, stunned. Arden got up with his fists doubled, prepared to strike again. His father grabbed him from behind.

"Let me go!"

"Arden, Arden, you don't know what you're doing! That's First Speaker Rowen you've just struck down. Please. Don't cause any more trouble."

"That's Rowen?" Some of the others were sitting up, as if the spell had been broken for all of them. "Friends! We have Citizen Rowen among us. The great Rowen himself!"

Rowen? His name was passed among the youths as if the sound of it was something strange and amusing. Someone started to laugh; in a moment, they were all laughing like madmen, some of them staggering across the sand on all fours. Arden leaned against his horrified father.

"Silence! Silence, all of you!" Parry cried. "Have

you no respect? Have you all lost your minds? Shut up! Shut up!''

Rowen shook his head, trying to clear his senses. Parry, who had been shocked by Rowen's actions, now looked ready for violence himself.

"Speaker! You're cut!''

"I'll be all right. Just get your boy home.''

"Thank you, Speaker. But what about these others?''

"Let them do as they please,'' Rowen snapped. As he left the beach he could hear their laughter against the sound of gentle rain.

Rowen had planned to meet his wife in Weiring proper, at a small inn they were fond of. Shaken by the incident at the beach, however, he had taken a floater up to a grove of gum trees tucked in a gully near the top of the terrace, far above the city. It was getting dark now that the wall fluorescence had begun to ebb, and from the mouth of the grove Rowen could see the curved string of lamps along the Weiring waterfront and, out on the lake, blue and amber running lights on the trawler fleet. Thunder rumbled from miles overhead. Probably the weather front had climbed well past the Midlands terraces by now.

Rowen sat down wearily on a bench in the shelter of a glass gazebo and tried to comprehend what had happened on the beach. It wasn't the ridicule that bothered him; years of politics had made him almost immune to it. What concerned him was the way the mindlinked youths had focused on him. Something had directed them. Something had been mocking him through the bodies of those people on the beach.

The groupmind. One thing was certain: Rowen had seriously underestimated its power. Group consciousness was like a cancer forming polyps all through the body of the Citizenry. They were few and isolated now, but how long would it be before the body started to falter, before the cancer took it for itself?

Sinom was laughing at me. It was Sinom.

The rain let up. Rowen left the gazebo and walked to a place deep in the grove where a metal slab jutted from a clump of bleeding heart. Here was the block the Citizenry had voted him last year. Other such blocks, some very ancient and in questionable operating condition, had been carried here from the homeworld. This one, Rowen's, was the first installed on Conteirre, and for that reason, to break precedent and make it possible for the honor to be awarded to others, Rowen had accepted his.

He ran his hand over the beaded raindrops on top of the block. A few keystrokes and he would be drawn in, incorporated into the crystalline structure of the metal. He sighed and knew there was no longer any possibility of his resigning.

A branch snapped behind him. Startled, he turned and saw Mehga standing beneath the copse at the entrance to the grove. The sight of her relieved the oppression he felt.

"Mehga! I'm sorry. I'd intended to return to Weiring before you arrived. How did you find me?"

She kissed his cheek. "The Harbormaster told me."

"Well, I'm very glad to see you." Just then Janoo crashed through the trees and landed on Rowen's shoulder. The Xein had been fishing in the lake, and gripped its catch in several of its claws.

"Mehga . . . forgive me if my thoughts seem unorganized. I had planned to tell you something at the inn, inform you of a decision I had made. Now . . . now . . ." He shook his head. "I just witnessed something that chilled me to the bone. Some kids on Weiring beach, mindlinked, with the tide about to drown them."

"You were going to resign, weren't you?" Her voice sounded strange, remote.

"How well you know me! Yes. I had convinced myself that after seventy years the Citizenry was as tired of me as I of them. No more inspiration to give. No more inspiration required, really. But now I realize I was wrong. We face more challenges than ever before, challenges that seem easy compared to what we have already faced, but which are in reality much more difficult. I cannot abdicate my responsibility now. Please don't think it's out of any lack of confidence in your ability to govern. It's just that I must stay. I'll need your help—all you can give—to keep the Citizenry on the right path."

Something flashed in the dusk. Rowen realized that Mehga was pointing a dart pistol at him. He laughed in shock and disbelief.

"This is no time for playing, Mehga!"

"It's you who plays, husband. Your impulse is to destroy what you don't understand."

"Are you mad? Has Gaelen poisoned your mind at last? Give me the gun!"

A dart quivered in the ground between his feet. "Gaelen is as insignificant as you, Rowen. An errand boy, nothing more. I've been with the Mother this afternoon, and she has helped me to see her vision of the future. A glorious future! She led me to a place I've been searching for all my life, where power and meaning are real, not just slogans. It will be my task to help the Citizenry find it as well."

"Mehga, listen to me. Today Tyron showed me something at the dig above Meems. It was a warning."

"Tyron has already volunteered to be the first to occupy a suspension cell, as an example to his fellow Citizens. And now, husband, if you will be good enough to turn around."

Suddenly Janoo buzzed toward her, claws out. Mehga shot at it, missed, but managed to knock it down with her fist. Before it could right itself she stepped on its carapace, pinning it helplessly to the ground. Calmly then, she opened a panel and yanked out its power cell.

"Mehga! We have been husband and wife!"

"That means nothing to me now, Rowen." She brought her pistol up.

Rowen stared at her. Her eyes were calm. Then, suddenly, she reached over his shoulder and punched a code into Rowen's funeral block. The block began vibrating, locking his arms, sucking him in. He screamed her name, but there was no one there to hear him.

A flash of magnesium-bright light curled the petals of the bleeding heart bush. Of First Speaker Rowen, all that remained were footprints in the wet earth.

Mehga considered the situation. After a moment, she received her instructions, turned without remorse, and left the grove.

Book Two

THE TWINS

CHAPTER 4

Jesse James Wallace leaned against the piss-stained wall and lighted his last cigarette with his next-to-last match. He was cold. The thin windbreaker he wore was no protection at all against the salt wind funneled through this back alley off the perpetual marsh that bordered Morgantown and covered most of the rest of this miserable planet. Faintly, Jesse could catch a few notes of music from the clubs along the main street: Just a few hours ago he'd been inside one of them—couldn't remember the name, nor did he care to—warm and happy with a big pile of chips in front of him and a table loaded with suckers to match. But things hadn't worked out. He'd made his pile alone and, all by himself, lost it, the proceeds of two weeks' hard work at the tables. Jesse was still stunned by how quickly things had changed for him. One minute he'd been looking for a good roll; now he was looking for somebody good *to* roll. He had to have some money to get off Morgan, and to make a stop at the convent where he'd left his sister.

Jesse decided to swallow his pride. The Morgantown gig was supposed to have been a solo—that's the way he'd wanted it this time—and until tonight, things had

27

more or less gone his way. But he needed his sister's help now, and he was sure Katya was watching him. He took a deep drag and framed the familiar summons in his head.

Kat? Got one for me?

There wasn't a response right away, and Jesse felt a surge of fear. Had she cut him off at last? It was inconceivable that she'd ever do that, though he knew he'd given her cause lately.

Come on, Katya. Please. How else am I gonna get back to you?

No.

The cigarette fell from his lips, and he didn't care. He felt like an amputee waking up and discovering someone had reconnected his arms again. But the relief lasted only a moment, replaced by outrage.

What are you talking about, no? You wanna stay with those chanting freaks the rest of your life?

Get money some other way. I won't help you rob anyone by force.

Didn't you see what happened to me in there?

They switched the dice on you. I'm surprised you didn't know better.

Well, thanks one hell of a lot for telling me, huh?

Solo, remember? You wanted to make it on your own.

Jesse grimaced, perfectly able to visualize his twin sister's smug expression. So it was going to be one of her "I told you so" numbers again.

He considered how to beg without it looking like begging—tough, when she knew him so well. But just then he heard footsteps coming from the mouth of the alleyway. It was hard to see things clearly in the murk, but Jesse could tell that the man was very well dressed—and drunk. To hell with Katya anyway.

Thanks for nothing, Kat. Maybe I'll get back to you later.

Don't do it, Jes, you don't know who—

His sister's projected voice sounded alarmed, but Jesse didn't care. He cut her off, closed his mind to fur-

ther reception, and moved into the shadows of a doorway. The pigeon was lurching toward him. It wouldn't
take much to put him down long enough to relieve him
of his goods.

"Come on, sucker," he whispered. "Just another
couple steps." Jesse saw his mark pass under a shaft of
cold light from one of Morgan's three moons, and for a
moment he thought there was something familiar about
the guy's face. If he hadn't been so cold, or so pissed off
at his sister, that might have made him hesitate. As it
was, Jesse wiped his hands on the legs of his pants and
moved out. In a second he had the man by the front of
his coat and was slamming him hard against the alley
wall.

The mark groaned and went limp. Jesse eased him
down, let go, then started through his pockets. Right
away he found the biggest wad of bills he'd ever seen in
his life—nothing smaller than C-notes, the whole roll
bigger around than his wrist.

See this, Katty? Not too shabby.

Nothing came back. She was probably still pouting,
not that it mattered. She'd come around; she always
did.

Jesse opened the guy's vest after he'd stuffed the cash
into his waistband. Inside the inner pocket he found an
evil-looking weapon with a pistol grip and a ruby tip
that looked like it could draw blood—the kind of gun
that fired an oscillating beam. It could reduce a man to
gumbo or shake down a ten-story building—heavy ar-
tillery for such a respectable-looking citizen.

The mark began mumbling something.

"Shut up, Pops," Jesse snapped, finding a thin wallet
in the other vest pocket. Incredibly, his victim laughed.

"I said shut up! Otherwise I'll have to put you
away."

"You jus' bought yerself a shitload of trouble"—
belch—"kid."

"You don't know what the hell you're tal—" Jesse
stopped when he flipped open the wallet and caught the
name on the mark's ID. He looked again, hoping he was

seeing things, but the name hadn't changed.

"Dink Morgan! *You're* Dink Morgan?"

Dink Morgan belched in Jesse's face.

"Jesus Christ! What the hell are you doing running around alone at night?"

"Don' know. Never anybody dumb enough to try rollin' ol' Dink before." He listed against the wall like an old sack of flour. "Ask m'boys. Lookin' fer me right now."

"Swell. That's just swell." Jesse straightened Morgan up a little, then brushed off his coat. "Uh, look, here's your money back, okay? You just forget you ever saw me. Waddya say, Mr. Morgan?"

"Naw. Don' forget faces."

Jesse looked at him. Morgan's eyes were half glazed over—but the hard glint behind the alcohol told Jesse that Dink Morgan truly would not forget, that he would repay this insult in full if he ever caught Jesse on his planet. He decided he would need that money after all. Morgan, however, clutched it tightly in his piggy little fist.

"Come on, give me that."

Morgan laughed. For the moment he was having the time of his life, and Jesse found it impossible to gain enough leverage, even with one foot on Morgan's belly, to pry loose even a single finger. Just as he got the idea to prick Morgan's hand with the tip of the oscillator, Jesse heard more footsteps from just outside the mouth of the alley.

"Boss? You back there?"

Jesse modulated his voice and yelled back, "Yeah. Takin' a leak. Be right there." Then he pointed the oscillator at Morgan. "You just keep quiet for a minute and everything's cool."

"Sure, kid. Run all ya want. I'll find ya."

"Okay. Remember I gave your money back."

"Hey!" At least three of Morgan's men came running at him out of the fog. Jesse aimed the oscillator and tried to get off a shot, but he had no idea how to get the thing to work. Cursing his bad luck, he beat it around the corner onto a quiet street of closed shops. One end of it emptied into the marshes; the other into an L-shaped cul-de-sac without even an awning to climb. The street coming off the L fed back to the casino strip, but sure as hell Morgan's goons already had that one covered. Jesse closed his eyes and prayed.

Come on, Sis.

Too long. He closed his eyes and breathed the hated word through tightly clenched teeth.

"Please."

Her response was crisp, and so clear she might have been standing next to him, yelling in his ear: *Use the ogee.*

Ogee? Jesse knew they'd be on him in a few more seconds.

Oscillator gun. There's a safety cap on the side of the handgrip—flip it open with your thumb. That's right. Fire at the left-hand building. There's people sleeping inside the ones on the right.

Jesse closed his eyes and pressed the trigger. The ogee buzzed in his hand—and then there was a roar as the warehouse at the end of the alley collapsed, blocking any pursuit with a jumbled pile of mud bricks.

All right, now what? I can't seal off the whole friggin' street.

You won't have to. Morgan's limo is sitting on a pad out on the marsh. His pilot's the only one aboard.

Limo? Listen, Katty, local transportation's the last thing we need right now . . . Katty? Katya! Jesse stomped his boots on the muddy cobblestones. Wasn't it just like her to hold a grudge at a time like this!

But in the absence of any forthcoming advice, limo it was. Jesse sprinted down the street until the pavement ended and his boots began sticking in the salt clay. He was hot about his sister and the way she'd treated him. Why the hell hadn't she warned him about Dink Morgan? It always seemed like she wanted him to mess up just so she could have the satisfaction of bailing him out. Sure as hell she'd be saying "I told you so" as soon as Jesse picked her up.

Maybe I should take the limo and leave her in that convent, he thought. She'd soon find out how much she missed having him to do things for her. He might depend a little too much on her ability to see things he couldn't, but there were two sides to that particular coin. Anyway, maybe that's what was holding him back in the first place—depending on her advice too much. He had half a mind to run out to Morgantown port and grab the first flight off-planet he could get—alone.

Unfortunately, he'd been stupid enough to hand Morgan his money back.

Jesse stood at the edge of the water and peered into the fog. No sign of a limousine, or even of a pad—only the waving tips of sawgrass that grew thick on either side of the boardwalk extending past the end of the street. Unwilling to go back the way he'd come, however, he went out a little farther just as a gust of wind lifted some of the mist.

He understood then why Katya had cut him off when he'd complained about "local" transportation, because Morgan's limousine was anything but that. Dart-shaped and sleek-hulled, her tail bulged with a cluster of eight induction engines. But she had more going for her than that. Evenly spaced along her midline were brilliant silver bubbles that Jesse recognized as VQ generators —nodes that enabled the limousine to punch straight courses through curved space. It was the most beautiful, compact starship Jesse had ever seen.

He made sure the ogee was ready, steadied his nerves, then boarded the ramp.

"That you, Mr. Morgan?"

The cockpit was set above the main deck, which had all the comforts—scaled down—of a salon in a planet-side mansion: a wet bar, pull-down bunks, even a buzz-chair for nights when Morgan didn't feel like going into whatever port he was in for entertainment. A full complement of navigation and communications gear was stacked into the cockpit level. Jesse checked back in the engine compartment and saw he was the only other person on board besides the pilot. Things were starting to look better.

A couple of stabs at the hatch controls got it secured.

"Mr. Morgan?" The pilot hopped down. He wore a sling with an ogee just like the one Jesse carried, but he blanched when he saw Jesse's pointed at his head.

"Let's have the belt, friend."

The pilot unclasped it and handed it over. "Where's Morgan?"

"Sleeping it off. Now get back upstairs. You've got work to do."

"Who says so?"

"I don't mind flying this heap myself, pal." He waved the gun. "Take your choice."

For a second, Jes thought he might actually have to shoot him. The pilot cocked an ear, hoping to pick up the sound of reinforcements. All he heard was rustling sawgrass.

"Okay. Have your fun. Where to?"

"Circassian convent," Jesse said, following him into the cockpit.

"What?"

"Circassian convent."

"I'll need the coordinates, pilgrim. That's not one of the boss's usual hangouts."

Jesse opened his mind and reached for his sister. He wanted coordinates from her, and to tell her he was on his way. He felt the dizziness that usually signaled contact. But then, abruptly, the connection changed, as though someone had cut into the line. He felt a chill, and a presence, *something* that was watching him, something that was interested in him. Then, abruptly, it ceased. Whatever it had been, Jes knew that his sister had not picked it up.

Am I going nuts? The pilot made a move, but Jes got the ogee up in time.

"A-6 and the mine road, that's where it is. Now move it!"

CHAPTER 5

Katya Belle Wallace tried to keep her mind on scouring the blue tile counters of the convent kitchen. She told herself not to worry; that the break in contact was something Jes had done. She wound up using way too much cleanser. Jesse had blocked her out many times, but this had been something else, something with power that Jes could never have.

Katya sluiced the excess grit from the counters with a bucket of fresh water. In spite of her uneasiness, the break was not without its irony. After all, it was Jes who'd demanded the two-week separation. "Alone," he'd said. "No interference. No sisterly help. That's the only way I'll ever get something going for myself." Then, as usual, he'd struck trouble and called her. Soon they were going to be together again.

But right now, temporarily at least, they were cut off. Katya was frightened. She wondered how her brother felt.

They had been linked since they were six years old, when they'd been taken from the happy comfort of the orphans' home on Aurica to the harsh mining colony on Hexxan. There, in the shadow of tailings tumps a mile high, they'd lived with a nervous woman named Frieda.

Frieda's husband had wanted kids. Frieda had no idea what to do with them. However, she soon sensed that Jesse and Katya were different from the sorts of children she read about in books, and she responded the only way she knew, with punishment as harsh as the oxygen-poor wind of Hexxan.

Jes she left more or less alone, fearing his possible retaliation. But little Katya had been subjected to a bewildering onslaught of beatings, verbal abuse, and incarceration inside a storage shed outside the house. There, enduring hours of darkness and the insane howl of winds shaking the sheet-metal walls, Katya had learned to touch her twin with her mind and hold on. She needed an anchor. Jesse became one.

From the first, he'd resented it. He still did, even after he'd established his role as the one who could fit in with normal people, the one who took care of arranging things. That started suddenly one day when Katya sent her brother a taste of pain after a particularly vicious beating. Calmly, Jes had gone to the kitchen, got a flatiron, and brained Frieda with it. Then he'd freed Katya, and together they'd gone to the Hexxan port, where their looks and wretched clothing convinced a sympathetic tanker captain to lift them off-planet.

Thus their career started. First as a beguiling pair of moppets, headed by the quick-witted, surprisingly sophisticated boy who was in turn infallibly guided by his sister's nose for a soft touch; later as a con artist saddled with an introverted twin sister, never staying anywhere long, never allowing outsiders to get very close. Always running. Always strangers. And now it would begin all over again.

Katya turned out the kitchen lights and went to her tiny room to pack. She could not communicate with Jesse, but she did sense the ship he had stolen, and it was only a few minutes away. There was just enough time for Katya to thank the abbess for her kind hospitality. To find her, Katya entered the cloister and stepped outside to the hedges that bordered the convent night gardens. On Morgan certain plants unfurled their broad, pale leaves only when all three moons flooded the marshes with their dead, shadowless light. The convent gardens were full of these night orchids, carefully tended by the abbess herself.

Katya hoisted her duffel bag and halted near a gap in the hedge, looking for the abbess so she could ask permission to enter. As always, the holy woman found *her* and spoke first.

"Leaving, are you?"

"Jes is on his way. I just wanted to thank you for having me here."

"Well, come in."

Stepping through the hedge was like entering another world. Sheltered from the wind, fluted leaves the size of klaxon horns bobbed in stately rhythm. The abbess's wheelchair was in a corner, its occupant bent low, tending seedlings whose leaves seemed to emit short-lived sparks. I'm tired, Katya thought.

"Precisely," said the abbess. "Where do you intend to go now."

"I never know. It's up to my brother, I suppose."

"Yes." The old nun wheeled around, and Katya saw that she was wearing a heavy dark veil in place of the usual white. "And what will you do?"

"Help him. He needs my help. Maybe now he'll realize that we belong together. Anyway, thank you for letting me stay. It almost . . . almost felt like home here."

The abbess took her gloves off and shook them out. "This place isn't for you. You like to run."

Katya stiffened.

"I believe you'd run even if you didn't have a brother. Would you like to know why? I'll tell you: You're afraid of what you are. Oh yes! Your wayward brother Jesse is only an excuse."

"He needs me." Her voice was almost indignant, but the abbess continued in her soft, melodious way, unaffected by Katya's defensiveness.

"No, my dear. You need *him*. Without him, you'd be

forced to face your responsibilities. Oh, I was like you
once!'' She put out her arms, so that Katya could see
her thin, almost blue hands and wrists. ''We cling to our
flesh. But ages passed before this body ever existed, and
ages will pass long after the dust of it is gone.''

''I can't believe in God, if that's what you're talking
about. I've tried reaching God. There's nothing to
reach.''

''If it's any comfort to you, I don't believe either.
God doesn't exist yet. But God will. Will you permit me
to show you?''

Katya could sense the movement of the vortex all
around her, as if the garden and the cloister and the convent itself had begun to move. The attraction was
powerful—and dark. Only the sound of reaction jets—
Jesse's stolen limousine—enabled her to pull free of the
current. The abbess chuckled softly, shaking her head.

''But it's not the time now. Farewell, my dear. We'll
meet again when you learn what it is to *fight*.''

The abbess turned and pushed her wheelchair past
Katya and through the opening in the hedge. Katya
wasted no time following her out. She felt that the holy
woman knew about her and Jesse. It made her shiver to
think so, but surely that made no sense, when the abbess
had been so kind to her! Just then she saw the com-
mandeered ship land at the foot of the hill beyond the
convent orchards. She sucked air through her teeth and
started for it.

Jes, you and I have some serious talking to do.

It took her a few minutes to reach the landing site.
By then, Jesse had marched the pilot out. He now lay
face down with his hands behind his head, a sight that
shocked her so much that she dispensed with greetings
and came right to the point.

''You can't kill him, Jes! We need him to run the
ship!''

''No we don't. Give him the once-over.''

''I will not!'' She reached for the pilot's arm. ''Sir,
please get up.''

"What do you think you're doing, pal? Down!"

"Up, down, what the hell," the pilot said, resuming the prone position.

"Shut up. And *you* get in that ship." Jesse pinched the back of Katya's arm and swung her around and up the ramp into Dink Morgan's limo. After barking a warning to the pilot, he scrambled in after her and shut the hatches. Without a word to his sister he went up to the cockpit to try and start the engines. The deck rattled as the inductors opened up—and shut down almost immediately. There was a moment of silence.

"Kat, could you come up here a sec?"

Katya sent him a picture of just what he could do with his invitation. There was no problem with the circuit between them this time. Red-faced, Jes stuck his head out the cockpit hatchway.

"I didn't kill him, did I? I mean, he's one of Morgan's people, and they're gonna be after us. Katty? Look, Kat, I'm sorry, okay? I'm just a little nervous. Can't you find out how to fly this thing?"

"No."

"Okay. Have it your way. I mean, they'll get a fix on us in an hour or two and send, oh, five, ten guys to get us. You'll have your hands full then, sister dear."

Katya sighed. As much as she hated to admit it, he was right. Without looking at him she went up to the flight deck. A moment's concentration provided her with the details of the ship's control systems from the still prostrate pilot outside. She apologized to him after she got what she wanted, and told him to get away from the ship's exhaust. Then she took a blue data wafer from a stack between the seats and loaded it into the navigator.

"This is a prerecorded orbital trajectory. Take the overlock off, activate the navigator—here"—she pointed—"then fire the jets manually."

"Thanks, sis." He strapped in and followed her instructions. The limousine shuddered, then lifted off to streak across Morgan's triple-lit sky. In less than ten minutes they were safely in orbit.

CHAPTER 6

Katya stared out a port at the moon-triplet rising over the curved amber limb of Morgan. There were two brilliant, cratered companions which orbited each other, and a smaller, lozenge-shaped misfit that shot around the planet twice a day on a low orbit. Soon tidal forces would break it up. It was sad to see it move almost desperately ahead of the placid twins in their high orbit. They were linked together, and beautiful, and safe.

She was thinking of that when Jesse came down to the salon. He sat next to her, looking over her shoulder awhile.

"Beautiful view from up here," he said. It was lame, but it was an opening.

"Jes—" Katya halted, wanting to be calm. She managed at least to lower her voice. "I want to know how all this happened, Jes."

"I don't know."

"You don't *know*? Jes, you clobber a stranger, steal his ship, almost kill his pilot, and you don't *know*?"

"Hey, calm down! What I mean is, I was doing great. I was on a roll, must've had a quarter million Cs sitting right in front of me. And the dice were dropping just like I had an invisible hand, shoving the numbers right over." He shook his head. "Then, all of a sudden, my luck went out the door. Just like that. Six hours and the whole bundle was gone."

"So that gave you the right to steal."

"Dink Morgan wasn't gonna miss that bankroll."

"That doesn't make any difference! You would have attacked anybody who came down that alley. It could have been some old lady! Oh, Jes, what's happening to you?"

He stood up, pointing to his chest. "You wanna know what's happening to me? You wanna know? Maybe I'm fed up! Maybe we're finally starting to outgrow each other!"

"Oh, Jesse—"

"No, you listen for a change, lady. I had a chance to do some thinking down there. Some real, serious thinking. I had plans for the money I won. That's why, when I lost it, maybe I went a little crazy." He sat down again and took her shoulders in his hands. "But hey, we've got this ship now! That's what I wanted the money for, a ship. Last week I met a guy in the casino, said he was running an operation out of the Dwaeleone Rings—we were there for a while six or seven years ago, remember? Anyway, he said I should look him up and he'd see about fitting me in."

"Exactly what kind of 'operation'?"

"Some kind of chemicals. He wouldn't say and I didn't ask. Stop pressing your lips together, Katya. It doesn't matter how I get money, it's what the money's *for* that's important. I want to make it so we're safe and happy and never have to go anywhere we don't want to go again. Is that so bad?"

"Yes, it is. Running drugs is bad. I won't have anything to do with it."

"But that's the beauty of the whole setup! I'll be doing the work, taking the risk. Taking care of *you* for a change. You won't have to get involved at all."

"Jes, this is crazy!"

"No! All I can see is that you can't stand letting go of me. It's really a trip for you, ain't it, Katya? Compared to you I'm a cripple, a little boy, always getting into trouble his wise, powerful sister can fix! What a superior feeling that must be! I wish to *hell* I knew what it was like to be so superior. Look into people's brains. Know all, see all." He laughed bitterly.

"Oh, why don't you get off it! Do you think I want to be this way? God, if I could change it, Jes, I would. But I can't. That's just the way it is, and if you and I are going to be around very long, we've got to accept it." Her voice softened. "You used to accept it."

"That's just your trouble," Jesse said disgustedly. "You've always just wanted to accept. Accept! Think of what somebody with a little ambition could do with that poor little brain of yours."

"Someone like you, you mean."

"Damn right."

They glared at each other. Katya said, "And then what? You tell me, Jesse Wallace!"

"We wouldn't be having these problems. We'd be on easy street."

"Maybe you would. I'd be long dead."

Jesse looked hurt. "I would've taken care of you."

"I don't think so. You have a convenient way of forgetting things."

"Yeah? Well I sure as hell wouldn't have beat you into the ground every chance I got. Man, that sinks it! I'm taking this can to Dwaeleone, and you can do whatever the hell suits you when we get there. And lay off the mental stuff! I don't even want to hear that prissy little voice of yours with my *ears*, got that? Freaking—"

The rest of his angry words were lost in the buzzing of the proximity alarm system from the flight deck. Jesse turned pale and thrust himself forward.

"Holy shit, they're coming at us!" he yelled. "Katty! How the hell do you get this thing into overdrive?"

"Energize the VQ generators. Here." She came up behind him and threw the switches that charged the virtual field around the ship.

"We ain't moving, lady!"

"We have to feed a destination into the navigator."

On-screen was the ringed exhaust halos of at least half a dozen patrol ships. In a moment they'd be in range to use their oscillator beams. Jes flipped through the wafer stack, tossing blue disks all over the cabin.

"Where's the one for Dwaeleone?"

"We're not going to Dwaeleone!"

"Damn you, Katya, you want us zapped? Morgan'd as soon cook us as let us get away with his ship."

"Anyplace but Dwaeleone!"

"Here! Here it is." He had the wafer he wanted, and reached to shove it into the navigator. Katya pulled him back. Cursing, he swatted the side of her head, then, for good measure, punched her in the solar plexus. Nausea rose to her chest and throat. *All right, bastard, you asked for it*. She focused her mind and let him have a blast of pure, fresh hatred that sent him reeling back away from the panels. Before he could answer, she reached for the red lever marked VQ ACTIVATE.

Dink Morgan's limousine grabbed the chord path that offered the least resistance and followed it to its conclusion somewhere close to the red, ancient center of the galaxy.

Book Three

W'RING HARVEST

CHAPTER 7

Once it had been possible to stand in a boat floating in the middle of Lake Alissia and look up past the cluster of penstocks called the Palisades, past the stacked terraces out beyond the lip of the canyon itself into the soft pink of the Conteirrean atmosphere, and catch a noontime glimpse of the golden sun called Azor by the people who had taken refuge in its warmth: sea and earth and sky in one breathtaking vista reaching toward the center of the heavens.

Time had moved heaven considerably closer to the sea.

Heaven was now a vault of ice spanning the canyon along its entire length. The people living beneath this frozen arch had never known their sun. They knew only that sometimes when the high mists parted it was possible to see bands of dark and light that supported the faintly glowing creaminess of the span. Then, when the weather turned exceptionally clear, it was possible to catch a glimpse of the spume called Heaven's Gate—a hole in the sky that let through a torrent of holy waters from the places beyond heaven where the sky gods who had made the world lived. For a distance below the vault this tremendous flow was a roaring cylinder of purest white; but as it fell, the mighty currents of warm air rising from Alissia battered it into a spreading fan of mist whose rainbow-hued ribs sublimated away tantalizingly close to the place where the people of W'ring lived.

The fan was known as the Mother's hand. And this morning, to a stripling called Luci, the hand seemed an answer to a special prayer of hers.

"She hears us, Rav," she said excitedly to her companion. "I'm sure the Mother hears us!"

Rav's sleek head bobbed above the waves as he watched new currents blow the rainbow fingers into a pointed shape. "It's only water," he said, speaking with his mouth and dispensing with the hand signals they used under the surface. "There's a sea above the sky that falls through a breach. Just like the springs from the cliffs there."

She shook her head impatiently, tossing bright droplets from her fine, brass-colored hair. "How do you expect the Mother to hear us when you talk so much blasphemy?"

"Luci, for today—just for today—let's not talk about it?" He watched as she instinctively touched the silver band around her neck, the one that identified her as a future bearer of children. He himself did not wear the complementary bracelet of fatherhood and never would. That had been decided at the Grove two weeks ago, when the priestess Tahr had selected the finest girls for mothers and a few boys who would in a few years sire many children to play in the Alissian Sea. That Tahr had passed him over did not surprise Rav, but Luci had been devastated. Ever since, she had wasted her time with hours of prayer to the Mother, hoping that the priestess would name one more sireling, name the boy she had loved all her life to be her husband.

The alternative was something she didn't want to think about. In the distance, close to the bouys and pinnaces that marked the underwater towers of her home city, the sea was alive with children at play, tumbling and breaching in the warm blue waters. A familiar scene, one Luci and Rav had been a part of all their

lives. Yet now the play of the older striplings was sub-
dued. Like Luci, their activity was a shadow of itself,
motion carried on from habit and without joy. Very few
of Luci's friends had been chosen by Tahr in the grove.
Soon—they all knew it—the Mother's hunter ships
would land on the Alissian Sea to seek out and capture
young unbanded striplings of the proper age, taking
them in their silver holds to Meems, the city of the
Mother just below the frozen sky.

Sea mothers gave birth every two years. It had been
that long since Luci's nurse had taken her and the rest of
her crèchemates and locked them away for almost
three days. When she was finally released, her older
brother Poins and three of her cousins were gone. None
in her syb had been willing to speak of what had happened—indeed, to do so invited the wrath of the Mother
herself, who had the power to stop the rich flow of
warm seawater from the great Veins that came down
from the walls of the world. Such a disaster had befallen
the Pelyshemi to the south. It was said that their
priestess had refused to surrender a boy who was her
own son. Thus, the sea in their territory had turned
black and cold, had become a desert, and the neighbor-
ing seafolk had turned away those Pelyshemi who attempted to escape the Mother's vengeance. All had
died.

It was for this reason that Luci prayed so hard. Even
if Rav was unconcerned, worried only about crawfish!
They swam northward, far now from W'ring. Luci kept
stopping to look back, a troubled expression on her
face.

"Only a little farther, Luci. There's a sand lane where
they'll crawl into our baskets." He winked at her. "And
a sea cave for us."

Suddenly he arched his back and disappeared beneath
the surface. Luci blew water from the lung vents
beneath her arms and followed him through a waving
thicket of black and yellow ribbonweed, startling a
whole school of darters as she strained to keep up with
his easy speed. For a moment she lost sight of him and

suffered a flash of panic. But then the ribbonweed ended like a curtain dividing the rooms of a house and she could see him floating above a rippled meadow of fine white sand well crowded with crustaceans searching there for worms. Luci chirped softly at him as he went to work filling his baskets. It took but a few minutes to fill her own.

"What did I tell you?" he signed. "And I know a place where the wild lemongrass to season them grows."

"And where might that be, sir?"

"It guards the mouth of that sea cave I told you about." He chirped comically, then shot away, leaving only a bubble trail to mark where he had passed, but this time making very sure she could catch him.

They lay cradled in the lemongrass together for a long time while Rav dozed. As they'd made love, Luci had almost been able to forget that soon Rav would be gone, that she would be forced to mate with a boy who was Tahr's choice and not her own.

She watched the chain of tiny bubbles that rose from the corner of Rav's mouth as he slept. Rav was an air breather—rare among their people—born with an extra pair of lungs that he could inflate with air without the risk of burning their delicate tissues. This had never proved to be a handicap—indeed, Rav was stronger and faster than any stripling his age, and he possessed more stamina than many sires twice his age. But Luci had wondered many times since the ceremony in the Grove whether the defect might have influenced Tahr's decision—whether the priestess feared the spread of this trait among the W'ring.

It wasn't quite clear in her mind yet, but the thought kept coming: Rav was the only W'ring boy she knew who could survive out of water for more than a few hours. In that way he was like the sky gods in the nursery stories from the time before the Mother had come to care for the world. Then there had been no hunter ships, and sires and mothers and nurses lived in the sky, sometimes venturing beyond heaven itself to travel among

the great fire globes which glowed to show the way
through the void, to places, worlds, that had no rocky
walls to confine the ones that lived there. And Rav was
like them: strong and courageous, and even though still
a stripling, blessed with a far-seeing mind. Everyone in
W'ring knew it, and Tahr must have seen it too. Why,
then, had she not awarded Rav his bracelet?

*Mother, if you have not heard my prayers before, I
beg you to listen to them now. It's said that those taken
by your ships come to be part of you in the sky. I believe
this is true, and that to be called to your side is the
greatest blessing you can bestow. But your people need
Rav. Is it not possible that you have created one so
strong in body to be your constant servant here in the
sea? Grant the humble request of your servant and
motherling: Touch the mind of the priestess Tahr. Show
her your will is to grant my Rav the bracelet of
Fatherhood.*

Luci felt the power of her plea expanding, gaining
strength—only to collapse. *My Rav*, she'd prayed. *My
Rav.* The pronoun had robbed her prayer of its building
majesty, turned it into something base and unworthy. A
cold dense current seemed to spill across the floor of the
cave, causing Rav to stir. Luci looked at him and felt as
if the intrusion had frozen her heart.

A sign then, Mother. Not for me, but for him.

Rav was tickling her with a stalk of lemongrass, smiling at her in his relaxed way.

"You're harder to satisfy since Motherhood," he
signed, grinning.

"Let's go back, Rav."

"Why? I have to finish the second part of my nap on
my belly."

"Please. It's cold here." She pushed herself away
from him and drifted through the grass out through the
cave mouth. Rav was frowning when he caught up with
her. They both breached the surface at the same time,
throwing a plume of mist into the freshening afternoon
breeze.

"You know, Luci, sometimes you make me glad I

won't be here much longer.''

"Don't say that!"

"Well when you act this w—" He stopped, the anger suddeny gone from his face, and stared beyond Luci toward the north.

"What's the matter?"

"Don't you *feel* it? A vibration, coming through from the Palisades."

Stunned, she realized that she had been feeling it for some time: a deep, metallic pulse that could only come from machinery.

From hunter ships.

"There, can you see them? Gathering in formation." They looked like silver coins strung across the waterline, though at this distance—the Palisades were at least twenty miles away—it was hard to make out their true size or shape. They didn't seem to be moving."

"Oh, Rav! Will they come to W'ring now?"

"I don't think so. They'll work the waters around the Palisades first, but it won't take them long." He reached for her hand. "I'm glad we had this day, Luci. Whatever happens to me now, I'll never forget it."

"No!" She dipped beneath the surface to wet her lungs—and to hide her tears. "We can't give up hope. Surely the Mother will hear our prayers."

"She hears nothing!" Rav said fiercely. "She doesn't need your prayers, Luci, she only needs bodies—*our* bodies! Mine to consume so that her life will be sustained. Yours to breed like a stockfish—"

"Stop this!"

"—like a *stockfish*, Luci, to bear a dozen fine, healthy striplings for the hunter ships to harvest every other year. Do you think it would have made any difference if I'd been named a sire? Your precious Mother! Tell me what sort of precious Mother does such things to her children." He spat into the water. "*That* for the Mother!"

"Rav!"

"Remember me well, Luci, when you see the last of your children swallowed up by devils!"

"Where are you going?"

"Never mind. Go back home and pray."

"But there's time yet. We can—"

"No time for me. The Mother doesn't want you to have me."

He spun, about to dive. Luci's head ached with the pulsing of the ship engines, with the thoughts that raced through her brain. She touched the spun-silver collar on her neck.

"Rav, wait!"

He glanced back with a look of contempt. Luci hesitated, then ripped away the clasp that secured the collar. Rav watched, wide-eyed, as she hurled it away. It glittered and spun in its brief flight, before disappearing forever beneath the waves.

"Luci . . ."

"I won't be a Mother if I can't have you," she said, scarcely recognizing the sound of her own voice. Rav came to her, and the two of them became one again. "We'll let the hunter ships take us together," she whispered. "To Heaven together!"

"No," Rav said. "Not to Heaven."

"What do you mean?"

"Don't look so frightened! I mean I have no intention of being caught by a hunter ship, and neither do you."

"I don't understand."

"You will." He let the basket straps slip from his muscular shoulders. "Here, take the crawfish back to W'ring. I'll see you tomorrow morning." He dove, then popped up to the surface a few moments later. "Better put this back on for now," he said, giving her the silver collar.

"But—"

"No buts!" Rav grinned, stroking her cheek with the back of his hand. "It won't do having your crèchemomma locking you away. Trust me."

Then he disappeared for good.

CHAPTER 8

Rav swam east with a racing heart, scarcely able to believe what Luci had done. Upright Luci! For a girl who believed in the power of the Mother the way she did, removing that collar had proved both her love for him and her courage.

It also meant he must change his plans.

He had been planning his escape for months now, even before the grove ceremony, because he had been certain the priestess would never select him. How many air breathers had ever been sires in W'ring? Rav knew of none, and doubted he would be the first. Therefore, as the time for the hunter ship harvest approached, he had begun to train, one or two hours a day, guided by the stories he had heard concerning the ships' capabilities and methods of harvest. It was known, for instance, that no one could swim fast or deep enough to escape their mobile seines, which moved as if they were alive and could eventually entangle even the most determined fugitive. Nor was it possible to hide from them for very long, no matter how dense the sea forest or secluded the cavern might be. There were devices aboard the ships that allowed their crews to see through solid rock. Once the quarry was located, the hunters dropped weighted projectiles which released incapacitating drugs. No, the hunter ships stayed until the last unbanded stripling had been swept into their holds before they traveled far to the south, across the black-water desert, to the place where their harvest were transported to Heaven.

There was no hope of escape *in the water*. But out of it? Rav had sought out W'ring's oldest residents, people who had seen the ships come and go fifty times or more. None could recall witnessing a hunter ship or its crew leave the Alissian Sea to pursue a stripling. Why should they bother? Sea people could not breath dry air for more than a few hours before their lungs started hemorrhaging. But besides that difficulty was another serious problem: They spent their lives in the water, in a state of neutral bouyancy. Muscles that were strong for swimming were little use on land when one had to fight gravity and a body that became impossibly heavy to move. Legs were meant for kicking, not walking, and the best a beached W'ring might manage would be a painful shuffle.

It had been that way for Rav the first time out of the water. He'd felt as if an unseen hand was pushing on him, trying to mash him into the sand. After a few minutes he'd retreated to the sea in tears. But he'd kept at it day after day until a whole different set of muscles had developed, and he was able to stand upright, to *walk*. Soon he was able to travel beyond the beach to the verge of the desert, past the ruins of the ancient city which in times past had been a port, but which now stood well away from the shore, silent, strangled by the pink sands.

His experience had taught him other things besides the pain of physical training. For one, Rav discovered that his unprotected flesh was ill suited to extended periods in the dry. After suffering painful burns—indeed, he'd feared his hide might crack and spall off his body in inflamed chunks—Rav had obtained some oil-rich lotion from his old crèchemomma and used this in combination with wetted cloaks such as were worn in W'ring during holidays. Then, for the first time in his life, Rav had suffered thirst. The dryness in his throat had been an annoyance in the beginning which Rav dismissed as an unfortunate effect of lung breathing. But on longer forays the dryness weakened him. In the sea, of course, his body was in osmotic balance with its environment, and thus Rav had been unable to understand the cause of this terrifying affliction, which no increase in the amount of lotion applied or wetting of garments seemed to cure.

The answer had come, miraculously, on a day when he was dangerously near collapse and had stopped to rest near a freshwater stream running across the beach. Something about the water attracted him, until, suddenly, ancient instincts had forced him to take water into his mouth and *swallow* it like food. Never in his life had Rav tasted anything so delicious. Now he made a point of drinking at every training session, whether he became thirsty or not.

Thus he had trained, increasing the duration and distance of his excursions, until he became confident of his ability to survive on land for a day or two. His escape plan was simple enough: Rav intended merely to go into the city ruins when the hunter ships arrived and remain there until they left. After that his intention had been to fetch Luci from W'ring and travel north beyond the Palisades to another territory, living as best they could away from cities and superstitious obeisance to the Mother.

But Luci's action had changed everything. Now that the collar clasp had been broken, the ships might well harvest her along with the others. That meant that somehow Rav had to bring her to his hiding place until the danger was past, until they both could return to the sea.

Rav reached the place where the sea floor rose to join dry land, a little to the north of the ruined city, where a long wooden quay provided a mooring place for the work barges whose crews attended to various construction projects needed by W'ring. Many of the building materials the crews required came from the sea forests

and underwater quarries, but there were certain sub-
stances—glass was the most important—whose fabrica-
tion was beyond the skill of W'ring artisans but which
existed in abundance in the ruins above the beaches.
Several times Rav had observed work crews venture
toward the jungle with their carts. None were air
breathers, but instead wore a kind of breathing apparatus fed from small water tanks carried on their
backs. With them it was possible to remain on land a
long time.

Rav intended to steal one of these for Luci.

He surfaced some distance away from the end of the
quay. It was beginning to get dark, but Rav could see a
crew hoisting sails on a loaded barge. Once they finished, they would swim ahead of it carrying guidelines
to keep rudder and sails in trim.

One of the crew removed his breather, tossing it into
the barge. The others, when they were finished with the
surface work, simply tilted their mouthpieces back
behind their heads before diving into the water. When
the barge cast off, Rav saw there was nothing left on the
quay. Cursing his foolishness for believing the breathing
tanks would be left untended—especially now, with the
hunter ships on their way—Rav set off after the barge,
staying in the turbulence behind her to avoid being
detected, gaining on her little by little.

I'm lucky the wind's not stronger, he thought, suddenly feeling weary and famished. But his determination gave him strength, and a few minutes later he was
gripping the barge's slippery rudder. A single powerful
kick gave him impetus to clear the low transom. But his
foot caught in a coil of rope as he climbed aboard and
he fell heavily onto the deck.

"What the hell—" Two of the swimming crew peered
over the prow at him, but it was too dark for Rav to find
the breathing tank immediately. "What d'you think
you're up to, boy?"

There it is! Rav reached underneath a tarpaulin and
yanked the breather free by its strap—just as crewmen
were climbing aboard to grab him. They were old, most

of them, and Rav thought he could outdistance any pursuit in spite of his fatigue. But just to make sure . . .

He drew his glass knife from its leg sheath and cut the mainstays. The sailcloth snapped into the faces of the crewmen closest to him. A moment later Rav was back in the water, laughing and swimming faster than he'd ever swum before.

He put the breathing tanks in the little cave where he'd hidden the rest of his supplies. Then he headed back to W'ring—and to Luci.

CHAPTER 9

Three hours subjective time after Katya had thrown
the VQ field onto the hull, Dink Morgan's limousine
popped out of chord in a high equatorial orbit above a
large planet whose hue and marking roughly resembled
those of Mars. Longitudinal cracks, some running pole
to pole, divided the surface. The planet orbited a main-
sequence yellow dwarf star. None others could be detected in any of the bands available to the limousine's
navigator because of the extensive and relatively hot
shroud of hydrogen and dust surrounding the system,
which reradiated energy in long wavelengths.

Jesse Wallace checked the charge indicators and
slammed both fists to the panelboard in disgust. Below
was a planet of canyons separated by deserts rippling
with marching sand dunes. Mars had been like that
once, but Mars had been landscaped; Mars had had
people on it, cities. Mars was a frigging paradise compared to this cheeseball.

"Lovely. You sure know how to pick 'em, sis."

"I didn't pick it." Katya reached over him and
ordered the navigator to display a list of chordable
destinations, given their remaining charge. It considered

the problem a long time—too long—until Jesse entered the command again. This time they got an answer:

> NO PRERECORDED ENDMASS AVAIL
> ENTER ALTERNATE WITHIN .56 PARSEC SPHERE

Jesse groaned. "Half a parsec. I can *throw* this thing half a parsec!" He rubbed his eyes. "All right, what's our position?"

This time the response was swift:

> CHORD TRACE ABENDED

"I'll restart the sequence," Katya said, trying not to sound worried.

> FILE CHORD TRACE DOES NOT EXIST

"Does that mean we're lost?" Katya said.

"Of course it means we're lost! What the hell do *you* think it means?" He glared at his sister. "You're really something, you know? A whole friggin' diskpak of destinations and you send us here."

"We could be close to an inhabited world. Let's just jump out of here."

"Without a ref? You must be nuts. I'll take this over some stinkin' black hole any day. Man, this is the end!" He was getting worked up. "Always gotta have your way no matter what. Well, now we're marooned. Can your talented little brain appreciate that? We're stuck, and we're gonna orbit till we eat the last of Morgan's canned pâté."

"Jes—"

"Shut up." He turned away, pulling into his shell like a hurt little boy. Katya wanted to slug him. By now her brother had convinced himself that *she'd* taken the ship, *she'd* forced him to fly off-planet with a dozen militia ships in pursuit, and now *she'd* purposefully dumped them here just so she could have the satisfaction of staying in control. It wasn't rational—but then, neither was Jesse at the moment.

Then she saw the mirrors as they popped over the horizon like shards of glass on a beach.

"Jes!" She leaned forward, increasing screen magnification. There they were lined up along the eastern brink of a particularly wide canyon, their frames bent and twisted; some of the reflectors that had cracked and spalled off into the sand drifted around their footings. But they were there, definitely artifacts, definitely signs of life.

"Let me see that!" Jesse switched to the wide-angle sensors. "Look at those grids. There's hundreds of square miles of 'em. Must be some kind of heat exchange system. Hold it—is there a thermal band on this thing?"

"Right here." Katya shifted the controls and suddenly heat-red showed between the gridlines like squares on a checkerboard. "A lot of it looks dead."

"Yeah, but something's pumping down there. See if you can get the sensors working on some readouts."

"Okay." The mouth of the canyon was directly below them, but about all they could make out visually was a band of green well below the planet surface. Katya watched the analysis data as it came up. "Water vapor, molecular oxygen, one and one half percent CO_2—"

"I like it! What's the green stuff?"

"Ice! Wait a minute, the canyon's deeper than that. There's a layer of ice two-thirds of the way up. Below it's warmer, wetter—I think I can generate a topographic map off the radar." She entered the command and suddenly a drawing materialized on the screen of the ravine in cross section: relatively narrow at the top, gradually widening to a maximum span of twelve miles at a depth of thirty miles—halfway down. The walls on both sides were scalloped into a series of shelflike projections every couple of miles. The vault of ice connected opposite shelves at a depth of eleven miles, and it was more than a mile thick itself in places.

"That must weigh billions of tons," Jes said. "I'd thought sure it was the bottom itself. How can it just hang there with nothing underneath?"

"Force dome maybe."

"Maybe." Now Jesse was smiling. "But do you realize what that means? Force domes mean power. Power means people."

"Not necessarily."

"No, but it means we might be able to charge the ship here. Katty, I want you to find out."

She reached for the sensor controls. "I can try to get thermal traces underneath the icecap—"

"Not that way." He pointed to his head. "Use your mind."

"No."

"What do you mean, no? You want to get out of here, don't you?"

"Yes, but—"

"Then do your stuff. You can make contact and explain who we are and what we want, and we can be gone in a couple of hours. What's the problem?"

Katya bit her lip. "Jesse," she said slowly. "When you were in Morgantown stealing the ship, we were in contact. All of a sudden, then, we were cut off. As if something . . . someone were blocking the signals."

"You were mad at me, remember? You just stopped talking."

"No, it wasn't that. I was worried about you. I *wanted* to stay in touch."

"So? You didn't."

"Jes, didn't you feel anything at all?"

He looked her in the eye and said, "No."

"Well, I did, and I know I couldn't have imagined it." The expression on her face showed she didn't quite believe him. He didn't want to give her time to dwell on that and spoke up quickly.

"Look, sis, you agree we've got a problem, no? I mean, we *are* lost, and we are low on fuel."

"Yes, but—"

"And you *can* scan, can't you?"

"Of course I can."

"Then I don't see that we've got any other choice. If something bothered you on Morgan, you've just got to forget about it and concentrate on the problem at hand. Look, if it'll make you feel any better, I'll come with you. If there's any sign of trouble, any whiff of something we can't handle, pull back and I'll chord us out of here myself."

"Promise?"

"Cross my eyes and hope to die."

She stared at him a moment more, still doubtful. Finally she relaxed. "Okay."

"All right! Come on in."

Katya closed her eyes and reached gently for her brother's mind. Jesse calmed his thoughts, waiting passively for the familiar, reassuring contact. It was strong and steady, the way it had always been before.

I'm right with you, sis. Just float us down nice and easy.

The sensation of out-of-body travel *was* like floating. Together, they drifted out of the ship, still aware of standing together on the flight deck even as they glided rapidly toward the surface of the planet. They passed the great mirrors and saw the machinery that had once kept them properly oriented toward the sun. They flew over abandoned vehicles that were surrendered to great red drifts of sand, and then into the polished upper levels of the canyon.

Are you getting this, Jesse?

Yeah. Something went wrong here, didn't it? That snowpack's got to be a couple thousand years old. Why don't we have a look at what's underneath?

Katya smiled. *All right, brother, get ready for the big drop.*

They started down seemingly at the speed of light, both of them whooping with joy, when suddenly his vision of the canyon clouded, then went dark.

His sister was gone. He called for her, but the darkness only closed in on his inner voice. All right, all right, now just hold on, he told himself. Freaking wasn't going to help. But it was bad to lose her like that; even worse, to realize that his unprotected mind was far from his body. Without Kat, there seemed to be no way to reunite them. He tried to move, concentrating as hard as he could. He got nowhere.

And then he heard the voice. It was soft, comforting, speaking a language he had never heard before, but which he could somehow understand. Gradually, as the voice reassured him, he became aware of a form draped in white.

Let me show you where your sister is, the voice said.

Now he saw a glittering point of light, as cold as frost. It grew and spun, and suddenly he was close enough to see his sister floating over him. She was as white as marble. Her eyes were frozen, and needles of ice capped her teeth. Shocked, he tried to embrace her, but she was just out of reach, and he had no way of moving closer.

The voice spoke. *Go to her. Save her.*

I can't!

The figure in white reached for him. Her touch was like fire. Fire that filled him up. Fire that, when he tried to grab Katya again, helped him move. He moved! He surrounded her somehow, and the fire inside him warmed her, brought back the flicker of life inside her frozen image. It took all his strength and willpower, but somehow, Jes was able to take her out of the canyon, back to the ship, back to the safety of their bodies.

Katya slumped to the floor.

"Katty! Katty, come on, wake up!" She was as cold as death. He cursed and chafed her wrist until she moaned. Then he took her down to the salon and filled Morgan's bathtub with hot water, got her out of her clothes, and pushed her through the seals into the tank. While she soaked, he shook and pinched and rubbed her arms and legs until finally her color came back.

"That's a girl. Come on, you're gonna be okay." He dried her off and put her into Morgan's bed. Finally, blessedly, she opened her eyes.

"Jes?" Her voice seemed centuries old.

"Yeah?"

"Take us out of here. Please . . . take . . ."

Then she slipped away into exhausted sleep.

Two hours later Jesse was staring at the navigator display. It told him he had three minutes to decide whether or not he wanted to go suborbital on this pass and make the descent to the mouth of the canyon. The display also included the helpful warning that if he did, there would be enough power remaining to achieve low orbit afterward—but not enough to charge the virtual field. If he took them down now, they'd stay down.

On the other hand, he could chord that half parsec out away from the galactic center and be pretty certain of winding up someplace within hailing distance of a working planet. The limousine had a distress beacon that could be picked up halfway to Andromeda. That might bring the cops, or even Dink Morgan's men, but maybe that was better than sticking around to face whatever it was that had hit his sister so hard.

Jesse rubbed his eyes. It was so hard to think straight. He kept remembering the sound of that pretty voice, and how the figure in white had energized him. For the first time in his life he'd been able to do what Katya could. Maybe it had all been a nightmare, a shared hallucination. But then how could you blame this planet?

REENTRY DECISION ENTER Y OR N

The navigator didn't care about what happened. It only wanted an answer. *Damn*. He could pull that drive lever right now and chord them out of here. But that would be the end of Dwaeleone, the end of his dreams of independence from his sister. On the other hand, if he took the limousine down and found a way to charge the cells, they could go anywhere they wanted. Anywhere!

REENTRY SEQUENCE AUTO CANCEL: 60 SEC
REENTRY DECISION ENTER Y OR N

Maybe Katya had cooked up the whole nightmare just
to scare him into doing what she wanted. But she'd been
so cold! And he'd been more frightened than he ever
had in his life. Katty wouldn't ever try to hurt him like
that. She never had before.

REENTRY SEQUENCE AUTO CANCEL: 25 SEC
REENTRY DECISION ENTER Y OR N

Jes looked at the navigator. He balled his fists. I'm
going down for a charge, he thought. Nothing else.
Nothing else. With nine seconds left he hit the yes key.

Thirty-five minutes after the burn was completed, the
limousine made a smooth, automatic descent into the
mouth of the canyon, over the mirrors, then down past
the first terraces jutting from the canyon walls. Whatever had existed on them was locked in a mixture of
water and CO_2 ice. Great daggers of it hung from the
edges of terraces on both sides of the chasm. Cloudy-
looking, knobby, and cracked, some of these tremendous icicles were five hundred meters long. They
shivered and rang with the whine of the limousine's
dozen jets, and some of the smaller ones broke off and
smashed against the curving green surface of the ice cap.
Now Jesse could see that this glacier was anything but
smooth. The tremendous compressive forces of trillions
of tons of ice had fractured its surface, throwing up
bluffs and mountains that would have made crossing it
on foot impossible. And there was running water as
well: great roaring gouts of it, streams that would have
dwarfted the mightiest rivers of Earth. These had cut
knife-edged channels deep into the vault in a pattern
that looked like fine lace from above. The source of the
flow was near the north end of the canyon, a vent where
water vapor from below condensed into a hammering
rain on the flanks of a frozen volcanolike cone. The

resulting streams headed south to feed a broad, glistening lake. There was a whirlpool at its center, releasing the moisture that had escaped. It was what probably kept the ice vault from collapsing, renewing the surface without allowing a fatal buildup of mass.

It was also the doorway to whatever lay below. With his charge running low, Jesse had no choice but to take it. The opening was irregular but several hundred yards wide at its narrowest point. No problem passing through it with the avoidance systems working. But it would ruin the jets to suck so much water, so he'd have to drop the limousine into the vortex and restart the engines once they popped clear underneath the ice cap.

The limousine skimmed over the surface of the lake, gaining altitude to avoid jagged mountains of ice and concrete that had spalled off the upper terraces. He reached the smooth spiral of the whirlpool and hovered in the spray. When the navigator showed the limousine centered on the vent, Jes reached for the throttles and cut power.

Water hammered the outside of the hull. He was afraid the noise would wake Katya, but then the ship began to tumble like a button in a box and he knew his sister wouldn't be going anywhere. Soft rainbow light came through the screens. Then the wheeling panorama turned into striated bands of pastel and green and phosphor blue. He pushed the throttles forward again. The engines sputtered, caught, sputtered again. By the time they got up thrust, a terrace was coming up fast. The ship flashed by what looked like a gigantic honeycomb, then inward over a snow-covered forest, slowing, but slowing too late. Jes tried to pull the nose up. The ship hit ice, bounced once.

The last thing Jes saw was the panelboard coming up at his head.

CHAPTER 10

Luci had a long, uneasy swim home without Rav, while the throbbing motors of the still distant hunting fleet made her head ache. Things that had been so simple an hour ago when she'd been in his strong arms now seemed horribly confused. Had she really torn her own collar off? Thank the Mother that Rav had been able to retrieve it for her. And yet his action baffled her when she thought of it. Had he not proposed that they defy the Mother together? Why then did he give her back the symbol of their separated destinies? Did Rav think she was foolish? Or did he believe she was incapable of formulating plans of her own?

Luci surfaced and looked in the direction of the ruined city high on the near shore. No sign of Rav or any other swimmers—only a barge crew struggling with a wayward sail. Rav, I need you now to tell me what to do. She wanted to pray with all her heart. But what would the Mother think of her prayers after what she'd done?

Perhaps she didn't notice. The world was huge, and there was much the Mother had to care for. Perhaps she hadn't seen the glitter of that silver collar as it entered the wave tops of her sea. Or perhaps she meant for Luci to remove it, as a test, a sign she approved of her love for Rav.

As if in answer, a hollow clap of thunder rolled through the sky, reverberating off the vault of Heaven itself, though there wasn't a sign of a storm. Pieces of the sky were falling, silver bits that glittered in the fading afternoon light. Luci's mind wanted to accept it as the sign she so desperately sought. But in truth, she had never heard thunder so immense, with such a bell-like character. Its harmonics were still tingling her ears.

Badly shaken, Luci swam the rest of the distance to W'ring as fast as she could.

"Where've you been!" Kehri was angry enough to bark the question out loud rather than sign it as Luci entered her crèche. The crèchemomma was very red in the face. To appease her, Luci offered the baskets full of craws that she'd carried from the sandmeadow.

"I've been gathering craws for dinner, Mum."

Kehri looked inside, her expression softening.

"There's lemongrass to go with them. I'm sorry it took so long."

"Supper's been fixed and eaten," Kehri said. "There's some left if you're hungry."

Luci flushed. Some of the other striplings who were still at the long glass table giggled at her. Others didn't look so happy, but Luci was aware of the tension here. Obviously her crèchemates had heard the engines of the hunter ships too. Seeing Luci's dismayed expression, Kehri smoothed the girl's hair, turning her back on the others so that only Luci could see the signs she made.

"You know, Luci, I was about to send some of the men out looking for you. We were afraid you'd done something foolish—tried to run away."

Luci made her eyes wide. "Why would I ever do that?"

"I think you know. I haven't told the others yet, though I'm sure most of them have guessed, but the ships will be here tomorrow. It's a time of happiness and sorrow for all of us who must stay behind. I've been at this crèche for many years, seen many of my children taken into Heaven by the ships." Kehri smiled. "I wanted to go along every time! But my duty was to stay here, raise more children to serve the Mother as she saw fit. Do you understand me?"

Luci remembered Rav's words. *A stockfish*. She felt shame for herself, and for him.

"Look at me, child." Kehri gently raised Luci's chin with the flat of her hand. "You have been chosen for the hardest thing of all. Children born of your own body will be taken from you. It is hard to understand, I know, but you must accept what you are, take the grace that the Mother sends you."

"Yes, Mum." She could see some of the other children trying to get a better view of the conversation.

"Tomorrow I want you to stay inside. Help prepare these beautiful craws. The children who don't go will need your help. That's part of your duty now, Luci."

Tears stung Luci's eyes as she nodded.

"Good," Kehri sighed kindly. "Now try and eat something."

"I'm not hungry, Mum. If you don't mind, I'd like to go to bed now."

Kehri smiled. "All right. Maybe sleep's what you need. I'll come for you early tomorrow, before the others wake up."

Luci went up to her niche in the sleeping room, but her thoughts, running like the freshets that bounded from the Palisades, would not let her sleep. Here in the safety of the crèche the duty Kehri spoke of seemed clear enough. And yet there were things on the shelves lining the niche that Rav had given her: a sparkling six-sided crystal, for example, threaded with a thong through a hole painstakingly drilled by him; a pearly trumpet of coral; and what had been his most prized possession, a gold coin embossed with the starburst symbol of the sky gods, a relic of the time before the Mother. Rav gave it to her when they pledged their love, made their vow to stay together no matter what.

But the priestess had canceled all vows when she gave

me the collar. Why hadn't she canceled their love as well!

She heard sharp, excited whistles as some of the other striplings came up to the sleeping room. Luci closed her eyes, pretending to be asleep, as some of the older girls spoke out loud.

". . . feel sorry for her. Tomorrow we'll be part of the Mother. All she has to look forward to is more work!"

"Aren't you scared, Seex?"

"Not if you're there. You'll hold my hand."

"Until the Mother takes it."

How lucky they were, she thought, not to have to face a choice like hers.

Luci waited until the waters surrounding the crèche had taken on the violet shade of night and the last of her excited crèchemates had fallen asleep before cautiously drifting out of her niche and through the windowway that faced away from the center of W'ring City. The luminous glow of rock lamps cast ghastly shadows which the darkness soon swallowed at the edge of the sleeping town. But Luci knew where she was going and used the soft evening currents as signposts toward her destination—the sacred grove of the priestess Tahr. Luci had decided she could no longer take the uncertainty, no longer weigh the factors alone. This time she was going to demand an answer from the Mother's image, which resided deep in the heart of the grove, in precincts given over to the priestess's care. To enter without Tahr's permission was audacious—and dangerous, for the priestess was a terribly strong woman with huge jaws and sharpened teeth which had killed tiger skates in battle.

But I have the right. Why else would the Mother have put such questions in my mind?

Luci entered a region of warm water that told her she was near the entrance to the grove, which lay inside a rich furrow beneath the W'ring outlet of one of the great veins that nourished the Alissian Sea. She felt lightheaded in its effervescent flow, pulled up, and drifted forward into the heavy copse of seafern and ribbonweed and iron-brown kelp whose leaves resembled daggers. Only a week ago this spot had danced with the shadows cast by a hundred sputtering torches as half of W'ring had come to witness the selection of motherlings and their future sires. Tahr had made her choices in the clearing just through the gates, her acolyte sounding a metal bell—which was said to be made of a part of the Mother's physical house—after each fierce call of a name. Now everything was dark, silent, as if the ceremony had never happened at all. Tahr must be waiting inside her cave, for she never left the grove. Luci hoped the priestess might be sleeping now.

She passed through the foliage and into the water above the clearing. Beyond, she could make out traces of a bright phosphorescence coming from the grotto where the Mother's image resided. Luci dared not pray, for fear of awakening the priestess; instead she gave a single strong kick that propelled her across the public temple and into the heart of the sacred place. The ribbonweed seemed to wrap itself around her arms and legs as she passed, perhaps in warning. But Luci chose to ignore their pull and broke free, making some noise as she tumbled into the second, smaller clearing.

There stood the arched glass grotto that housed the sacred image. Before it burned a sizzling fireball atop a tripod and brazier, fierce blue that hurt to look at as it spun and danced above—but never touched—the polished metal. The sea floor around the grotto was a bed of carefully tended pebbles. Luci was careful not to disturb them as she moved to the front of the shrine.

Inside it was the seated image of the Mother, wrapped in veils of purest white. Luci stared, uncertain of what she should be feeling. She'd expected to sense the majesty and power of the goddess, to feel diminished in her presence, *in awe*—but there was nothing, only the silent image, the bubbling fire, the somnolent warmth pouring into the grove from the vein outlet. Could the Mother even see her?

Mother, my mind is undisciplined and does not understand that it cannot have two things. Motherhood

*and wanting Rav are both in my nature, and I cannot
choose between them. Help me, I implore you. Spare
Rav. Allow him to serve you by siring the children of
W'ring. Or, failing that, then allow us both to be taken
into your body, where we might become a part of the
glory that is to be . . .*

Nothing. It was like a song sung in the deep confines
of a cave, echoing back but not escaping for others to
hear.

*Why won't you listen! I am one of your children!
Don't you understand what I'm feeling now?*

Perhaps the Mother could not see her. Luci took a
deep breath and approached the image. Its white veil
had been pinned with a jet clasp. Scarcely believing
what she was doing, Luci reached for it, released the
catch, began to draw back the silky cloth. . . .

"Stop right where you are, pup!"

The priestess! Her rough, gargly water voice stunned
Luci as much as a blow would have. She began to let the
veil drop but was pinned by the stare of a brown eye;
whether it was stone or flesh, Luci could not tell—she
could no longer say whether she herself was stone or
flesh; she could only feel the rush of turbulence caused
by Tahr's powerful approach kicks.

Tahr leaned against Luci's shoulder as she refastened
the Mother's veil. Then she turned the girl around to
face her.

"Lose something, did you?" She held up the silver
collar, showing her terrible row of teeth as Luci fran-
tically felt her bare neck.

"It . . . it must have caught on a branch," she stammered.

"Never felt the clasp ripped open either, I suppose.
Look at me, girl! Do you know I'm entitled to slay you
on the spot?"

"I meant no harm. I was only praying, priestess!"

"In the grove I'm pledged to guard with my life! I'm
priestess here only as long as I can defend it. When
another comes stronger than I, she'll kill me the way I
did Shamsis, priestess before me. Then the grove will

have a new guardian." Bubbles rose from Tahr's mouth as she growled, "Think it's you, pup?"

"N-no, priestess!"

"I could also kill you for profaning this grotto." Incredibly, Tahr laughed. "But this place would be a graveyard if I did every time a silly stripling thought to address the Mother directly."

"You mean I'm not the first?" Somehow, Luci felt disappointed.

"They come every other year. Though you're the first motherling I've seen without her collar. Most put their own skins first. Not you. Still hankering for young Rav, are you?"

"Priestess, I came to ask if we could both be taken together."

"I know, I know," Tahr said with an impatient wave of her hand. "The answer's no. I picked you for a motherling for good reasons, and I never change my mind. How would that look to the rest of W'ring? As for your lover, he's a sport—a throwback to our ancestors who never lived in the sea and lived to serve themselves and not the Mother. Some of his children would be born to breathe air, like him. Too much trouble at harvest time." Tahr yawned. "However, his strong body and vigorous mind will do well as part of Mother, and so he shall go"—her voice sharpened—"in spite of his plans."

"Plans?"

"He's an air breather, isn't he? Capable of living up in the dry. It doesn't take much to figure out what he intends to do. We can't have that, can we, pup?"

"He only wants us to stay together!"

"Together, yes, and out of the Mother's hands. We can't allow that. She needs Rav, just as she needs you to make other bodies to replace the ones that die. Hers is a precarious balance of life against death, and the loss of even one chosen stripling could mean her surrender to the abyss. Is that what you want? The death of the Mother because of your puppy love?"

"No."

"That's the result. And if the Mother dies, so dies the sea and the sky. Our world will silently freeze. Do you wish to be responsible for that?"

Luci blinked tears away. "What can I do, priestess, what can I do?"

"Allow Rav to believe you'll go along with whatever he plans to do to escape the ships. Feign injury—you'll know the best way—at the crucial moment, when the ships are closer to you than to the shore. This"—she fit the collar around Luci's neck, the way she had at the grove ceremony—"will tell the ship to keep you free. Rav will be taken, as was the Mother's intention."

"Betray him? Please don't ask me to, priestess. I'll stay inside my crèche—"

"No. He must not be permitted to escape. You'll betray him, all right, and one day you'll see the wisdom of it. The Mother's ways are harsh. But betrayal is how she came to power, and betrayal is the way she'll escape to greatness in the end. You are her servant, and, yes, you'll betray the stripling. Do you understand me?"

She forced Luci to look into her deep blue eyes and Luci heard herself saying yes—over and over and over again.

CHAPTER 11

The knife-sharp edge of the morning shadow rolled across the translucent sky of ice, dividing the high reaches into pearly dawn and long, reluctant shadows as Rav approached W'ring. He'd spent the night outside the city, away from his crèche, sleeping fitfully inside the hulk of an ancient skyship, *forcing* sleep for an hour or two because he knew he needed rest if he was to succeed today. To sleep, he had to battle his soaring heart: Every time he thought of Luci tearing off her silver collar, shimmering bursts of love mingled with disbelief rippled through his body.

He wished there was something he could do that could show even a fraction of the love she had shown for him. And to think he'd called her a superstitious Mother-fearer! No, Luci was fine, and incredibly brave. She would not be sorry that she'd forsaken Motherhood for him.

The thought had made him smile, because he realized that once they had avoided the hunter ships and were away from W'ring, there was no reason that Luci couldn't have children—their children, not the Mother's. Alissia was an ocean, after all, and they could find a place to raise a family where priestesses and ships could never reach. Surely there were deep pools where Luci could stay while he searched for food in the night.

Finally it had been too much to think about, and he'd retreated into a light, refreshing slumber. Awakening, he'd eaten a few kelp floats and taken a more serious attitude toward the task at hand. Before any of his dreams could come true he had to get himself and Luci away from the water ahead of the fleet—and it would be better to get out of W'ring as early as possible, before the hunt monitors took their posts on the perimeter.

W'ring was still quiet. Rav kept to the shadows along seldom traveled lanes until he reached Luci's crèche. Once its lacy archways and glass-tiled turrets had been a welcome sight for the stripling. The crèchemomma, Kehri, had always greeted him with a fondness—and with tasty snacks. Now it seemed forbidding, a prison for his Luci.

He hid himself inside a stand of tall horsetails growing along the side of the building and let out three sharp whistles. No response. Rav floated up closer to the sleeping room and repeated the call. His impatience mounted until he decided to go inside for her. But then he saw her at the windowway.

"Quiet," she signed. "I'm coming."

"You look beautiful," he returned. And in truth she did—her sleek body wrapped with white streamers that added grace and power to her movements as she left the place of her childhood behind. The white—a color reserved for Mothers alone—puzzled him as he followed her silently away from the city. But he decided that she had put them on to avoid any hint of her real plans.

When he decided they were far enough away from W'ring, Rav put on a burst of speed to catch up with her. Luci did not stop, however, and Rav finally cut in front of her and caught her in his arms.

"Luci, where are you going?"

"Away." Something about her voice was off as she stiffened against his embrace.

"I've been waiting all night for this. Haven't you missed me?"

She turned away. "Rav, I—"

"What is it? Luci, don't be nervous, everything's arranged."

"Yes, it is."

Why wouldn't she look at him? Of all days for her to act this way! He decided to be stern with her and had sharp words ready—when the water around them shivered with a powerful, throbbing rhythm. The hunter ships! The sound of their pulsating engines was much more intense than yesterday. Rav shot to the surface and saw a fleet of at least two dozen of the disk-shaped silver vehicles blowing clouds of spray near the north side of W'ring City. They held their formation for a few moments before separating in twos and threes on their rapid-search pattern. Rav stared, for though he had heard the passage of the ships many times inside his crèche, he had never seen their operation before. Each ship floated above the water, trailing ramps from sides and rear. At intervals, lozenge-shaped projectiles shot from tubes that opened along the prows. These moved ruthlessly and with amazing speed to snare those striplings who tried to dive away in fright. Already, netted children were being pulled along the ramps into the holds of the fleet. Even more frightening were the four ships that had settled into the water to take aboard the herd—yes, herd!—of docile striplings who eagerly surrendered to the Mother's mechanized harvesters.

Two of the ships skirted the southern perimeter of the city, increasing their speed and throwing great roostertails of spray as they cut the wave tops. Rav did not immediately realize their heading until the roostertails had grown perceptibly larger. When he did, he slammed back under the surface, his heart pounding.

"Come on, Luci, it's time to swim." Rav whirled desperately, unable to locate her until he glimpsed a flash of white streamer below on the seabed. A single angry kick brought him to her as the horrifying roar of the ship engines battered his ears. Luci was curled into a ball like a sleeping baby.

"What's the matter with you? Are you sick?"

"Go, Rav, there's still time for you to get away."

"No! It's together or not at all. Now damn you, girl, *move*!"

His strength became the strength of five as he took some of Luci's streamers in his teeth and swam for the both of them. After a few moments Luci's fright seemed to take hold, and she began kicking for all she was worth. The shore cave with its store of supplies and the breathing tanks for Luci wasn't much farther. But the ships were gaining on them. He heard her gasp and then stop.

"Luci!" The ships were no more than fifty yards away, engines throttling back now in expectation of taking another stripling aboard.

"You've got to get away, Rav." Her face was contorted by anguish. "Please!"

"We're almost there! Come on!" He tried towing her again, but she pulled free and grabbed his arm. She was doing something to the collar on her neck, taking it off, twisting it again and again around his wrist. Then she let him go as the huge, cold shadow of the hunter ships swallowed them. He could not untangle the twisted collar and the mobile nets came down, touching his shoulders, then parting, falling away from his body and leaving him free. But Luci—

Rav saw a trailing white streamer flash away from a bubble stream. The nets were taking her.

"Luci!"

"I'm sorry, Rav, I love—" Then nothing more, as the nets were pulled up the ramps into the ship.

Rav reached the surface, lunging for a ramp and missing as it closed against the hull. He could feel the engine throb increase. In an act of pure desperation he jumped onto the ship's prow, spread-eagling himself as it began to pick up speed. The metal was slippery, and there were no hand- or footholds other than a ridge of soft material that surrounded the edges of the hull, but he clutched at the seams in the hull plating and pounded with all his strength.

He could hear no sound other than the insane howl of

wind around him and the thrumming engines that carried them over the sea faster than Rav believed was possible. He clung to the ship by will alone, stunned, not knowing what else he could do. What had Luci done? They would have made the shore easily if only she hadn't stopped. Why had she been so afraid?

Rav cursed himself for letting her spend last night alone. The Mother-lovers must have gotten to her and filled her head full of fear. By the gods, he wouldn't let her go now, even if he had to ride all the way to Heaven itself, look the Mother in her eye, and spit in her hideous face! He'd do it, because he was right. She had to stop eating her children. Rav would make her stop.

He realized he no longer felt the ocean spray against his back. Chancing a look past the upper portion of the hull, he saw a sight no sea dweller had even seen before —the sea *from above*. The hunter ship had lifted away from the water and was following the slope of the first terrace. Already it had left the ruined shore city behind, and it was now passing rapidly over the sand desert.

The sea. From here it looked so narrow, dried-up in places north and south, snaking away into the distance until the horizon swallowed it. Rav looked, and for a moment forgot where he was, forgot what had just happened in the water.

Then the hunter ship banked, turning in formation with others that had also left the water with their holds full of bodies for the Mother. Rav clawed at hard metal, trying to stick, but the combined force of wind and gravity defeated him. He was peeled off, spinning in the air for what seemed an eternity. "I'm flying after them" was his only thought before he plowed feet first into a berm of hot, dry sand.

The last thing he saw before he lost consciousness was the arrow-shaped hunting formation completing their long sweep and vaulting upward toward the Mother and the sky.

Book Four

RESURRECTION

CHAPTER 12

Mother! My head hurts!

It was a long job untangling herself from Morgan's bed nets. When Katya finished she was out of breath and her temples were pounding, but she knew she was more or less in one piece. Then she remembered her brother and scrambled up to the flight deck.

"Jes!" There was blood all over the panelboards where he was slumped forward, and for a horrible instant she thought he was dead. Then his fingers moved. Fighting her way forward on the tilting deck, she reached him, eased his couch back, and saw the swelling and the nasty-looking gash on his forehead. When she touched it, he moaned softly and winced. His eyes opened. Incredibly, he grinned at her.

"Not much of a landing, sis . . . Sorry."

She breathed a curse and started down the ladder to the salon.

"Hey, where you going?"

"To get some ice for that stupid head of yours!" She found some in the cooler below Dink Morgan's well-stocked bar. There were also some clean towels, and, while she thought of it, a bottle of forty-year-old Armagnac. A drink from or a bash on the head with depended on what he had to say for himself in the next few minutes.

She was patient—under the circumstances. She cleaned him up and made him an ice pack for his bump, and let him have the bottle before she mentioned the obvious.

"You took us down, Jes."

"Yeah." He swigged brandy. "I guess I did, didn't I?"

"You can take us right back up again."

"I would. Except that there's no fuel for that." He saw her tense and added quickly, "But take a look out the rear screens. We've got enough to make it over there, sis."

The view was disorienting. Downslope, a mile or two away, was a city that had been reduced slowly to rubble by creeping rivers of ice. Beyond the smashed walls and listing towers Katya could see the faintly green, curving sweep of the ice vault, which seemed to reach all the way to the blue water at the very bottom of the canyon. Sandwiched between the ice and the water were green terraces along the opposite wall. On one of them was a large city, untouched by the ice, stretching along the edge of the terrace from end to end like a giant honeycomb. Looking at the city made Katya shiver without knowing why. She turned angrily to Jes.

"I can't believe how irresponsible you are! Wasn't what happened a couple of hours ago enough for you?"

Jesse calmly squeezed water from the ice bag. "You got dizzed when we popped out of chord. It happens."

"It wasn't the chord, and you know it!"

"Look, sis, I didn't feel a thing. Nada. Now we're down here, and the city's over there, and we can get all charged up and take off. If that's what you really want, I'd suggest you give me a hand clearing some of that snow away from the intakes."

"Jesse Wallace—" She stopped, realizing she wasn't getting anywhere. This was something new—him calm, her ready to blow up. The thing to do was settle down, be patient. Differences in brainpower aside, she had always been able to keep the upper hand in their relationship simply by outlasting him. All the same, she wanted to pound him.

Instead she went to Morgan's armoire and found a thick fur coat with double rows of gold buttons that were embossed with Morgan's initials. It flapped against her ankles as she took a pan from the galley. At the main hatch she got a readout that showed the air wouldn't kill her. Then she opened the lock and jumped down into dry, fluffy snow.

It was warmer outside than it looked. A few clouds scudded down past the lip of the terrace, curling against the supports for the next level before the draft sucked them away. Katya scooped snow away from the front engine pods and saw that the crash had done little more than dent the nose fairing. The clouds came more quickly as she worked, driven by frustration, and only when she paused for a breather did she realize that it was snowing again. Slow, feathery flakes fell on her face and hair.

Jes? Are you coming out to help me or not?

He waved at her from the flight deck ports. *Stand back, I'll try a blast to clear the rest away.*

Nothing unusual in their contact. Katya moved a few yards farther up the terrace. Jes had been calm enough. Maybe he really *wasn't* worried. Half ready to apologize, she reached for him again and got a view of the flight deck and the gauges on the panels in front of him.

The charge indicators showed power enough left for orbit. He'd lied to her! After everything that had happened, he'd lied! The inductors burst to life, and the limousine disappeared momentarily in a cloud of snow. When it settled, the ship was clear. Katya marched forward. They were going to settle this thing now.

Open that hatch, Jes!

Sure. Be right with you. If he sensed her anger, he was doing his best to ignore it. The hatch slid open. Jes stood in the lock with his hands in his pockets.

"Sorry I didn't give you a hand out here, sis. I was busy scanning that city for working power plants.

There's a few good bets on the periphery, and I thought we'd try the farthest one first. Wouldn't do to turn up in the town square, would it?''

"Why did you lie to me?"

"What are you talking about?"

"I'm talking about the charge indicators. We can orbit again and use the distress beacon."

He looked startled. Then his lip curled. "Spying again, huh, Katty?"

"I was *not* spying. Now I want an answer. What's down here that you want? What's worth risking both our lives?"

"There's no risk. We haven't been attacked, and we won't be."

"How do you know?"

"I just . . . I just know. You'll have to trust me."

She shook her head. "I can't trust you. Not until I find out what this is all about. We're not feeling or seeing the same things down here, Jes." Katya looked him in the eye. "You're going to have to let me come in."

"I told you. That's over."

"With or without your permission, I'm coming in."

He stepped toward her. "Sure you are! But why stop there, sis! Why not just take over complete control? Zap me. Burn me out so I can really be your puppet, and never give you any trouble again. Come on! What are you waiting for?"

Hurt and angry, she almost did it, focusing her mind sharply to penetrate his feeble defenses, then halting at the last instant. If she did that, she would be proving everything Jes had accused her of. She blinked her eyes, fighting tears, not knowing how to get through to him any other way. He smirked at her.

"I thought so. You really don't have the guts. Now get in here."

"No."

"This ship lifts off now!"

"Jes!"

He snarled at her, and then the hatch slid shut. A moment later the limousine's inductors burst to life with a deafening howl, blowing Katya back like a bit of paper in the maelstrom of churned-up snow. She spat snow out of her mouth, struggling to free herself from a drift as the ship disappeared.

"Jesse!" she called, repeating the plea with her mind. But she could not make contact. It was as though he'd suddenly ceased to exist.

For the first time in her life, Katya Belle Wallace was really and truly alone.

She sat for a time in the snow. A terrifying, desolate loneliness threatened to crush her for good. It would be so easy to simply lie down, close her eyes, let the snow and then the ice cover her. Maybe that was what the vision of that terrible coldness had been: a premonition. Her future. And Jes couldn't share it because he wanted to be free of her, on his own at last. He'd survive. He'd be better off. So easy to sleep . . .

No. There's danger here that neither of us understands. She couldn't simply abandon him. If they had to split up, let them choose a time and place that gave them both a chance for a healthy new life. Somehow she had to get him back. And to get him back, she had to survive.

Katya got up and started walking toward the forest. It was tough going because of a crust beneath the powder which kept breaking when she stepped on it. There was irony in this, she realized, after forty-five minutes of sweaty travel. Physical survival for both of them had always been Jes's department. It was clear that she was badly in need of experience.

Finally she got close enough to the line of trees that girdled the frozen city to make out dark branches through the swirling snow. Climbing atop a berm that ran lengthwise for several hundred yards along the terrace, she halted and opened her mind to call him again. The terrifying emptiness returned, but there was no answer from her brother. She called again, less openly this time.

This time she got an answer, but it was not from Jes. She wasn't quite sure what it was. Afraid she might be drawn again into the void that had swallowed her before, she pulled back, but the desperate voice hung on by a thread. It was faint, and it was calling for help, and the cry was the only coherent thing about the mad scramble of impulses and images that swirled around it.

The mind, however insane it seemed, knew that Katya could help. Abruptly Katya cut the thread and considered what to do. The mind was not a powerful one, merely strong with the strength of the desperate, lunging at one last chance. Was it a diversion? she wondered. Something to keep her from searching for Jes? Katya had sympathy for this being, whatever it was. But she decided that Jesse was more important. Once she moved away from this place the cries would quickly fade.

Katya jumped down into the soft snow in front of the berm, lost her balance, and stumbled back against its face. She hit a sagging framework that divided the face into rows of hexagonal cells. With an incredible crash, cells began shattering all around her. She covered her head with her arms, protected by Morgan's thick fur coat. Finally the noise stopped. She felt something dry and cold against the side of her cheek. She turned to a vision of grinning, yellowed teeth, leathered skin, deep, empty eye sockets, wild, brittle hair.

Corpses. Mummies falling all around her, holding their dead arms out toward her, laughing at her. Shuddering and suppressing a scream, she backed away through a vent of steam rising from one of the shattered cell openings. She was staring at the pile of dead men and women and didn't notice the steam nor the quick movement from inside the cell.

Only when the bony, warm, *live* hand clamped around her wrist and held tight as a manacle did Katya finally scream.

CHAPTER 13

The procession turned onto a broad, deserted avenue leading to the weathered dome of the Diet of Citizens. Leading it was a floating juggernaut flanked by open cars of weapons-toting bodyguards, along with several smaller wheeled vehicles carrying nervous-looking Delegates who had been pressed into joining the interminable progress from the First Speaker's residence to the seat of his power.

The grim-faced Speaker rode atop his tiered carriage like a gargoyle on a bronze wedding cake. He scowled at the boarded-up shopfronts and empty walkways, taking the lack of a welcoming crowd as an insult to his person. The Speaker may or may not have recalled the order of general curfew he had issued himself only the day before; nor did it matter to him that he had passed this street in this manner hundreds of thousands of times in his long, long tenancy of the Speakership. If they could not come out of love, then let them fill the streets out of fear. But the orders of the past few weeks had been contradictory, the Citizenry only reflecting their leader's uncertainty. They stayed inside, all but a few of them, to watch Gaelen's parade behind the safety of drawn curtains.

Gaelen himself watched as a female Citizen burdened with packages and a small child rushed from an alley. She halted when she saw the juggernaut, opened her mouth, then quickly dropped to her knees, forcing her child to the walkway beside her. Now, from speakers throughout the city, along the adjoining terrace, and from amplifiers mounted farther into the canyon came a sound that rocked the street: a recorded roar of acclamation louder than a million voices, loud enough nearly to shatter the ceiling of ice above Gaelen's head. Certainly witless with fear, the child's face contorted until the First Speaker's impatiently outstretched arm cut off the noise as if with a cleaver. The street, the buildings, the juggernaut itself quivered in the soundlessness; and only gradually was Gaelen able to hear the baby's wails. He stood up and projected a smile, an approximation of radiance from a youthful face framed in golden hair.

"Thank you, Citizens. Return to your business."

The bodyguards relaxed, cradling their weapons beneath their arms as the juggernaut lifted off and continued to the capitol. Gaelen's show of generosity only proved how seriously out of balance the regime and its ancient head were getting.

Things were more crowded in Chambers, where Delegates were easier to replace than workers, hence required to attend and provide an enthusiastic (and unrecorded) response to speeches that had been known to last as long as four days. Today Gaelen had been mercifully brief, stumbling through a disjointed account of the just completed harvesting operations in Lake Alissia and ending with an uncharacteristically distracted plea for unity and support of the Mind. It had taken no more than ten minutes, and when the First Speaker had turned away from the dais the Delegates had sat in stunned silence before beginning their hesitant, obligatory ovation.

Gaelen listened to it filter through the curtains that separated the Speaker's room from the rest of the Diet Hall.

"Oh, wonderful speech, Speaker Gaelen. Absolutely inspiring." It was a white-haired old woman with sagging cheeks and a broad red nose who said these things to him. Gaelen knew she was his parliamentary secretary, had been for more than eighty years. But the face meant nothing to him, and he could not clearly recall her name. Nevins? No, Nevins had been fifth, perhaps sixth before this one, and Nevins had been a man. But why, he thought, *should* he remember the name of this woman—even one who had served him for so long? In his term he'd employed twenty-five or thirty such people. Certainly, some of these had served longer than this one, and he could not remember their names either. Gaelen looked at her, and the vague fear struck him that he'd lost control of the muscles of his face, that his mouth hung slack, that saliva dribbled onto the perfectly polished top of the hornwood table he sat behind. He suddenly felt as old as he really was; open to the putrefaction and death he had been protected from for nearly three millennia.

"You don't look well, sir."

Is that true concern? Or is she afraid of what will happen to her if I die beside her now?

"Perhaps some wine." She hurried over to the sideboard for a decanter and a glass.

"Wine, yes, thank you . . . Sheeme."

"Mov," she said as she brought the amber liquor. She brightened when he sipped from the goblet. "I've just seen the manifest from the receiving hospital, Speaker. The take was better than four thousand this year. That should please your wife.

Gaelen's lethargy was broken. "Shut up!"

Mov turned pale. "I was only—"

"You've been secretary a long time. Maybe too long." He could feel his strength coming back in direct proportion to her fear. This was one game he'd never got tired of playing. He put his hand to the holster beneath his robe, feeling his heart begin to pound as the realization of what he intended to do hit her. She opened her mouth to beg for her life—

Then *her* signal buzzed from the door behind him. His pleasure evaporated, leaving a spare residue of disgust that was washed away in a surge of his own fear.

"Get . . . the hell out of here."

Mov was gone before he could even push his chair away from the table. Gaelen tried composing himself, but it was no good; there was no way to disguise what waited for him in the next room. Yet he felt no rebellious impulses. In spite of his fear, he had never once considered refusing *her* call. For, though he had been First Speaker ever since the time of the great Rowen's disappearance, he knew there were others who could play the role every bit as well as he.

The door opened as he approached. Gaelen took a deep breath and went through. When the darkness closed in on him he fought his panic, groping desperately for his chair or a bit of the wall—anything to prove to him that he had not in fact been swept out of his body and left to the mercy of the void. It was the same every time, and Gaelen suffered even as he cursed his own weakness. *She* would sense his fear and use it against him.

He touched something warm and soft. Her hair. Too late he snatched his fingers away as his wife's laughter flared and held, steady as a torch flame inside a tomb.

"Gaelen," she said. "That was a pitiful performance in Chambers today."

He let her pull him down to his chair. Now, as his eyes accustomed themselves to the room, he could see the outlines of her head and shoulders, set off by the pale aura that hugged the folds of her white robe. His wife was the Mother's intermediary—part of the Mind, but also of the Citizenry. Lately, now that the Mother devoted all her strength to anchor the Mind she controlled, Mehga had been granted considerable autonomy.

"I'm not well," Gaelen mumbled, repeating the words of his secretary.

"That is obvious even to Sinom."

"The pressure has been very great. Her demands for

more cells and bodies to fill them . . . it strains all our systems."

"If that were truly a concern to you, you'd have taken measures against the rebels in the Midlands." He saw her smile. "No, Gaelen, *pressure* is not the problem. The problem is that power no longer matters to you. Life no longer matters. I believe, husband, that you doubt the Mind will ever overcome the enemy. Isn't that so, Gaelen?"

Somehow he scraped together some defiance. "What does it matter? Anyone can see how we're bottled inside this damned trench!"

"Sinom wishes me to consider possible successors to the Speaker's chair."

Gaelen's mouth went dry. "The system still works. My reports show the latest harvest to be the best ever. What else can the old bitch want from me? I can't do anything about the Cold!"

"Save your breath, husband. I don't intend to see you fall. In fact, I'm prepared to give you a chance to redeem yourself."

For a long moment Gaelen said nothing. Death's appeal had deepened considerably of late. But not deep enough. "What do you want me to do?" he asked.

"Sinom has brought two off-worlders here. Twins. One of them, a girl child, has power. Great power, Gaelen; power the Mother craves. She wishes to use that power to break free of the Cold. Their ship has been reported south of Meems. I want that ship intercepted and the girl brought to me."

Slowly Gaelen smiled. "Are you saying you want to betray the old witch? After all these years?"

"The Mind is crumbling along with our world. It is too late now for Sinom, even if she does succeed in getting the girl to join with her. The fact that I can discuss this matter with you now is proof enough of that. Bring me that ship, Gaelen. It will do a little something to justify your miserable existence."

"And if I fail?"

"Should I waste threats on a dead man?"

"Probably not."

They laughed together—two laughs very different indeed.

The meeting with his wife vaguely excited him, but it wasn't enough to recharge his dissipated spirits. He returned to the Speaker's office and issued orders to his military command to track and capture the offworlder's ship. Then, as he always did when threatened by the emptiness, he cloaked himself in a plain, homespun cowl and left the Diet Hall alone for the receiving hospital.

This building was near the terrace edge, just above the great cell banks that nourished the components of the Mother's Mind. He entered it through a rear door reserved for his personal use.

Inside the air was hot and muggy, the cavernous interior alive with echoing sounds of splashing water, throbbing pumps, and the frightened yelps of the young harvest from the sea. This was the place where the water breathers were prepared for new lives as part of the Conteirrean groupmind. It was their clinical initiation into Heaven—thousands of bodies processed each year like cattle. Fresh meat for Sinom to chew for a hundred or two hundred years before she spit them out dead and called for more.

She didn't seem to care if Gaelen took one or two of the prettier ones in each batch on a slight detour.

He went up to the booth overlooking the main pool, signaling the surprised technician to continue with her work. The pool was crowded with bodies; there was no room for the water breathers to stretch out, or even to dip under the surface to breath properly. As Gaelen watched, more children slid down the chutes from the docking bays where the harvesters unloaded their cargo. They moved slowly along the slippery glass incline, writhing with contorted expressions when the technician activated powerful water jets to spray some life into them after their dessicating journey up from the bottom. Gaelen searched the faces with disgust. Most bore the phenotype of a breed meant to live out its life underwater: narrow, crested heads covered with slick dark fur; enlarged nostrils, and the rib vents for breathing water; huge, narrow-boned fingers webbed knuckle to knuckle with skin so pale one could see the delicate lacing of blood vessels inside. Creating the type had been one of the last great achievements of Conteirrean science before Sinom had swallowed it whole, and nature had embellished the work with modifications of her own. These were savages, fodder—and yet there was an innocence about them, a natural grace in the way they signaled each other with their expressive hands. Most were calm once the shock of the slide into the pool was over. Many even appeared eager for their coming union with Sinom. *Her* priestesses—the undersea equivalent of Gaelen's own Citizens' Police and far more efficient—had done their work beautifully.

A flash of golden hair caught his eye. In the far corner was a girl who appeared more robust than most of the others. She was frightened, but she controlled it well, and she even comforted several of the smaller ones who whimpered around her. Her creamy skin and firm, rounded breasts appealed to Gaelen, set off as they were by delicate ribbons of white tied around her arms and her narrow waist. Her eyes were as green as the sea, and Gaelen began to forget about the humiliating lecture from his wife.

"I'll take that one," he said. "Have her prepared and brought to my residence."

He watched as they fished her from the tank. It was, he decided, just what he needed to renew his energies for the breakthrough he knew would have to come.

CHAPTER 14

Rav tasted sand.

He rolled over and opened his eyes to light that wanted to burst his skull. His skin was raw from the fall into the sand. He sat up painfully and saw the shadow line falling across the western wall of the world.

The world as he had never seen it before.

Downslope, miles away, was the ruined city and the sea. Between it—how impossibly small the ocean was!—and the place he sat now was another ocean, a sea of pastel sand. Closer, glowing phosphor yellow, was the place where the terrace joined the real wall of the canyon beneath the massive underpinnings for the next level up. Rav stared at its dark underbelly and tried to comprehend this new way of seeing the world. He doubted his eyes, and yet, from that terrace the sparkling glass supports of a bridge—the one Luci had always called the Mother's Walkway—spanned the gulf to the green-banded shelf above the Palisades. There, downdrafts pulled air from inside the terraces, lowering atmospheric pressure and sparking precipitation that kept the land alive. Rav realized that if he were to live, he'd have to get across that bridge somehow.

He rubbed his eyes and looked at the whipping tail of

the great waterfall issuing from Heaven's Gate. Strange how the landmarks seemed so different when not viewed from directly underneath. For the first time in his life Rav sensed the true scope of this canyon, and saw many terraces that were more than banded shadows hanging from the milky sky. Each was as broad as Alissia itself. Could it be possible that other peoples lived on them as the W'ring did in the sea? If so, they must have cities, farms, perhaps hunters as well. Just below the sky, for example, was a glittering patch of tiny lights. Could this possibly be a city close to Heaven and the Mother? Perhaps that high terrace had been the final destination of the fleet. If it were true, Rav thought excitedly, then Luci was there, living and breathing, unaware that Rav was watching. Perhaps she had already been taken into the Mother's body, but it made no difference; in fact, it made speaking with her possible, in a way. Hadn't the teachers in his crèche told him to pray when he wanted to speak to departed crèchemates? Rav hadn't had much use for prayer these last few months, but he would make the Mother hear whether she wanted it or not!

Luci, he thought, with as much intensity as he could summon. I'm coming for you. Nothing's changed that we can't undo together. You saw my dream, I know you did. He remembered its horrifying conclusion and altered his wish. All but the last, Luci. We'll have it all but the last! Then he stood up tall and yelled her name to the sky, hearing it echo away aloft the hot, dry winds, before turning his back toward the sea and beginning his trek to the glowing canyon wall.

The sands of this desert were not baked in direct sunlight, but rather heated from below, and despite his land training, Rav's feet began to pain him. There was nothing he could do about it but push on; all his supplies had been left in the cave along the shore that he and Luci had not been able to reach. The sand was very fine, which made rapid progress impossible. Several times he lost his balance and fell back, only to struggle to his feet, covered with silt that rubbed abrasively against his tender skin, doggedly ready to tackle the next berm.

If determination alone were all that mattered, he might have crossed a thousand miles of desert this way. But his body soon let him know that will would not be enough. Will was nothing without water, especially for a stripling who'd spent his entire life living in it. Every breath he took, every drop he sweat, surrendered more water to the air. Rav tried to ignore the dryness in his throat, the tongue that suddenly seemed made of leather, by concentrating on the destination. But after a while the yellow glow lost its meaning—it was only a wash of color in front of his bleary eyes that refused to come any closer in spite of his determined efforts.

He stumbled more frequently now, not quite sure what was happening to him. Had the Mother somehow taken his strength without taking his body? Rav looked down on the twisted silver band still wrapped around his grimy wrist. She'd saved him—but not for this! Was it all to end here in this sand, his punishment for opposing the Motherways?

No! He reached the wind-sculpted crest of a dune, took another step—and tumbled head over heels down its sharp leeward side. For a moment Rav couldn't catch his breath and panic swept over him: Am I dead? But the sand was cooler here; when he was finally able to fill his lungs again he sat up to plan his assault on the next berm.

He blinked. Not ten feet away from him was a *claw*— a pincer such as craws had—sticking out of the sand. Luci, you've heard me! Rav half-crawled to the place, digging furiously to free it from the hot sand. A few yanks and he had it in his hands, ready to crack the shell and suck the juicy meat inside. But the carapace resisted his desperate pressure; and then Rav saw that this creature possessed a dozen pincers, all but one neatly folded against the outer rim of its disk-shaped *metal* body. Puzzled, Rav held the thing up and shook it.

A silver cylinder hung down from the bottom on some chords or tendons. Rav noticed an opening in the skin that was the same diameter as the cylinder. Curious, he turned the thing over and slipped the cylinder into it, pushing hard with his thumb when it became stuck three-fourths of the way down.

Suddenly two button things—*eyes*—rose on stalks from the center of the disk, swiveled around, and halted right in front of his face. So it was alive! And what lived could obviously be eaten, if only Rav knew how to open it. The eyes followed the movement of his right arm as Rav reached for the sheath knife on his thigh. He drew it—

The thing buzzed sharply and spun away. Rav dropped his knife in shock; he stared at it, then at the thing, before going for the knife again. The claw-thing was quicker: It whirled furiously and knocked the knife twenty feet away.

Rav scratched his head. Whatever this was, it was certainly smarter than the craws he was used to eating. And Rav could not remember having ever seen one fly like this thing could, either.

"All right, so maybe you want to eat *me*. Let's fight. Winner eat all." Rav giggled. It was stupid, talking to this creature, but he no longer cared. His thirst had progressed too far.

It buzzed again, then retracted its eye stalks. Rav got up on his heels. "Not fair that you have the knife. Twelve claws'll beat a knife any time." He laughed again, falling back in the sand as the thing suddenly launched itself into the air, buzzing away over the crest of the seaward dune. Rav watched it go, then saw the knife lying in the sand a few feet in front of him. He got to it, but no farther, collapsing and rolling onto his back with the last of his strength. A dream, nothing but a dream. He thought he could hear the laughter of children, smell fish gently poaching on a bed of phosphor coals.

I'm sorry, Luci . . .

Something thumped to the sand behind him, but Rav was unable even to turn his head. He felt cold metal against his lips, spatulas gently prying his mouth open.

Water came—cold delicious water trickling slowly
enough for him to swallow. The taste of it broke his
trance, and he shook his head, rolling over to see that
his benefactor was the claw-thing. Somehow it had been
able to sense his trouble and figure a remedy, bringing
water in a glass vessel such as were found sometimes
among the artifacts of the sky gods. Rav took the
pitcher in his trembling hands and poured it into his
mouth and over his face, washing some of the grit over
his parched body. He drank until he couldn't drink
anymore—then looked at the claw-thing and laughed.

"You wouldn't consider cooking yourself for me
now, eh?"

The thing shot a pincerful of sand over Rav's head,
then dug in warily.

"I suppose not. Well, how about some clothes, then?
You can see I'm not doing so well without them." To
Rav's surprise, the thing took off again, this time
toward the east. Rav shook his head. Surely this craw
wasn't able to understand human speech? His mind was
playing tricks on him, and yet there was the glass
pitcher, tilted in the sand in front of him. He took it and
breathed the rest through his water lungs, blowing out a
warm, instantly evaporating mist through the slits along
his rib cage. It energized him in a way the drinking had
not. Able to stand now, Rav started toward the next
dune.

He heard a sharp buzzing, heralding the return of the
metal animal. Suddenly it popped over the dune crest
and dropped a bundle at his feet. Rav picked it up, cut
the tapes with his knife, and unrolled a quilted garment
that wasn't a cloak, but rather had enclosed arms and
legs in the form of a person. There seemed to be no way
to wear it other than by tying the long leg tubes around
his neck and letting the rest hang down his back. The arrangement did not meet with twelve-claws' approval,
apparently, for it let out a sharp popping sound, rose
up, and before Rav could even turn, yanked the suit off
his body. It then laid the garment on the ground and, by

running a pincer along the front, opened a seam from neck to belly.

"Oh, you climb *inside*. All right, how's this?" He yelped as the thing scrambled up his leg to reseal the vent. When it was closed, Rav realized that he no longer felt the heat as before. In fact, contact with the strange material was quite soothing—almost as good as being in the water. Looking down at the way it fit his body, Rav remembered faded wall murals he had seen in places inside the ruins of the shore city. He had always imagined that the sky gods bore skins of many colors and textures; but now he realized that the images had been covered, as he was, with cloaks that fit like second skins. He himself resembled a sky god now. And this thing that had brought the water and the garment to him—had it been a pet to the gods, some kind of servant?

"I suppose I must thank you. Do you understand what I mean?"

The eye stalks twitched. What did thanks mean to an animal—if that's what it was—anyway?

"But I've got to go on. I need to reach that bridge up there, and get to that city at the edge of the sky. That's where the Mother lives, and where Luci is, and I'm going to get her. Loo-see, a friend of mine. The hunter ships took her to be with the Mother, and—oh, you don't understand any of this, do you?" Rav rubbed his chin, watching as the thing retracted all its pincers. It was as motionless now as when Rav had first dug it up.

"Well, even if you don't understand, thanks." Rav started off along his original course, due east. He had not taken more than a few steps when the thing flew at his head.

"Hey! Watch it!" Rav went forward again—and again the craw buzzed his head, raking a pincer through his hair as it passed. Now Rav's heart pounded. It hadn't occurred to him before to be frightened of this thing, and it was unpleasant to discover a deep-seated fear of things—animals—diving at him from above. It had circled and landed in front of him. This time Rav decided to go wide, circling a little to the north. The thing did not move. But as soon as Rav attempted to return to his easterly heading, it flew at him with a terrifying shriek.

Rav started running, with the flyer in pursuit, always to his right. Soon it occurred to Rav that the creature attacked only when he tried to veer in that direction. He pulled up, bending over with his hands on his knees, trying to catch his breath.

"All right," he puffed. "You win. Maybe you know a better way. I'll follow you if you promise to stay out of my hair." As if in answer, the thing spun off a spray of sand before saucering out and landing a hundred yards ahead. When Rav did not immediately follow, it jumped back half that distance, emitting a shriek that sounded very much like annoyance to the stripling. Having little to lose, Rav shrugged and trudged off toward the northeast.

Several hours later the slope of the terrace had increased to the point where the sand cover was almost gone and Rav walked mostly on hard stone. He saw the pincer-thing glide through a sinclinic formation folded into a narrow canyon along the fall line of the terrace. Feeling as weary as he had ever been in his life, Rav reached it and sagged against the smooth, steep wall at the entrance.

Here everything was yellow highlights and soft shadows overhead, where the massive support beams for the next terrace ran seventy-five feet above Rav. Inside the gully itself was a forest of narrow stone shafts, some taller than the masts of a sailing barge. They cast interwoven shadows that lay like a net over jumbled pieces of shafts that had toppled and broken. It was difficult at first for Rav to find the craw-thing amidst the wreckage. But farther back he caught the dull gleam of a metal slab and saw that his guide had landed on top of it.

Rav picked his way through the broken stone. As he crawled over a thick section that blocked his way, he noticed a pebbly finish covering its surface. Certainly it was too complex to have been carved either by moisture or by some unknown artisan. More than anything it resembled the rough, corky substance that sheathed the land plants along the seashore. Rav looked at some of the shafts that were still standing and saw that they indeed resembled the trunks of living trees. Yet they were stone. Back in the warm embrace of the Alissian Sea, Rav had been quick to ridicule any of his crèchemates, —and even Luci,—when they made claims about the power of magic. And yet how could trees be turned to stone? Rav moved more quickly now, as if by staying in this place he risked suffering a similar transformation.

Pincers hadn't moved from its perch on the slab. Rav put his hands on his aching hips.

"Where to now? We've almost reached the far wall."

It did not move. But when Rav tried to walk past, it grabbed his sleeve and buzzed excitedly.

"Here? Is this where you wanted to bring me all along?" Rav scowled. "I'm telling you, I don't intend to stay in this place—" Then he stopped, for the creature had done a curious thing. Flopping to the ground at the foot of the slab, it turned over on its back and made a whirring sound that Rav had not heard it make before, while at the same time raising one segment of its carapace. Extending one of its smaller pincers telescopically, it reached into its own body and withdrew a square chip of a substance that resembled the flakes of fool's gold Rav had collected as a child. The telescopic limb stretched out to Rav, and the thing buzzed impatiently until he took the chip from its gentle grasp.

Immediately it turned over, backed against the base of the slab, and thrust two of its pincers into a pair of holes just above the ground. When it did, the slab began vibrating, raising a cloud of dust that suffused more yellow light through the ossified shafts surrounding it. Rav looked at the chip. What am I to do with this thing? he wondered. Perhaps it's food of some sort. He stuck out his tongue to taste it, but the creature screamed at him, opened a mouth just below its eyes, and quite slowly moved its pincer from Rav's hand to the opening, repeating the action several times for emphasis.

"You want it." With an uneasy glance at the vibrating slab, Rav bent to insert the chip into the pincer-thing's mouth. Immediately he had to put his hand in front of his face to ward off the heat blast from the metal, which was beginning to glow even as a low-pitched whine seemed to rise from the ground itself. Rav backed away, tripped over a stone branch, then put his hands over his ears as the whine became a shriek that threatened to pierce his brain. Beyond the now white-hot slab, the petrified trees began to shiver with the intense harmonics, some of them shattering into heavy pieces that fell all around Rav, exploding as soon as they hit the ground. The shrapnel battered him. Rav screamed, "Stop it! Stop it!" Now the metal had so heated the air around it that it seemed to have become plastic, taking form as the sonic emissions wracked the stripling's smallest bones, tearing him—

And then it stopped. A single tree crashed where the slab had been, but the slab was gone.

In its place was a man dressed all in blue who spoke two strangely accented words: "Mehga, don't!"

CHAPTER 15

Choking thick steam frosted her eyebrows and hair as she struggled with the thing that had hold of her arm. Pull as she might, there was no way to release the grip. Even worse were the voices that came from the contact:—thousands of voices, pleading for help in hissing, alien tongues. Madness . . . the end of life . . . betrayal . . . laughter; bitter, hopeless laughter. It would destroy her.

She fought back.

It took all her will, but she pushed the voices away, then sent waves of soothing hope to the place they came from. Not for the sake of those desperate voices, but for herself. She brought the quiet down on them. I will help you, she told them, I will help . . .

The hand on her wrist relaxed. Steam cleared. Then a groan came from inside the shattered cell. Katya leaned closer, letting the hand slip from hers. She gasped. An old man—barrel-chested, with a hawk's face and hair the color of ashes—opened his eyes and tried to speak.

Please, stay still! Are you all right?

"No." A dry, tortured whisper in her own language. "Speak . . . words. Not . . ." He pointed to his head.

"Can you understand my words."

The old man nodded, and whispered, "Out of here
. . . help me to stand."

"All right." She reached in and put an arm around
his shoulder. Touching him, she realized that whatever
madness had possessed him when his cell shattered was
gone. His knees buckled when she got him out onto the
snow, but he was powerfully built, and after a few
moments was able to stand on his own.

"Oh, you're cold! Here!" Katya stripped off Dink
Morgan's coat. Then, seeing the old man's bare feet,
she helped him into her boot liners as well.

"Thank you, child," he said. His voice was sharper.

"We must find shelter. Do you understand?"

"Too cold . . . weak." She had to catch him as his
knees gave way again.

"A fire, then. You'll be able to move better if you're
warm. I'll get some wood from the forest down there.
Sit down. Wait. I'll be right back."

He nodded, and she stumbled across the snowfield to
the trees. There she found plenty of deadfalls with bone-
dry branches that snapped into manageable lengths.
Only when she was on her way back with the wood piled
in her arms did it occur to her that she lacked a means of
igniting them. Before, Jes would have thought of a way
to get the fire going. But Jes was gone.

She cleared a space in the snow away from the pile
of mummies and made a teepee of twigs, with bigger
branches around them. The old man watched in silence
as she stepped back, closed her eyes, focused her mind
like the beam from a magnifying glass. The wood
caught fire suddenly with a loud *whoosh*. Satisfied,
Katya stepped away to let the old man capture the
warmth.

After a few moments he said, "Useless."

"I can get more wood."

"Not what I mean," the old man snapped. "Tricks
like that. Useless and dangerous. She'll grab you right
up."

"Who'll grab me?"

"You know. You've known for a long time, haven't you?"

Wonderful, she thought. Mummies in a snowstorm, and now riddles. Katya stared at the fire until the old man spoke again.

"If you want to stay with me you'll have to keep your mind shut."

"My mind shut? Listen, old man, if I'd kept my mind shut, you'd still be in that cell."

"If you had kept your mind shut, you and your brother would still be together, girl!" His eyes glittered fiercely.

He reminded her, she realized, of a poem she'd read once, about an ancient mariner. "This isn't getting us anywhere. I won't do any more tricks, as you say, if you'll tell me where we can find better shelter than this. And while you're at it, how we can cross over to the green side."

"There is a power station on the other side of the trees."

"Do you think you can travel that far?"

"I'll have to, won't I!"

Her mouth opened. This old man was even more exasperating than her brother. All right, she thought. We'll see how fierce you are after a trek through that snow.

"Whenever you're ready," she said.

By the time they passed through the forest an hour later, Katya was exhausted. It was hard enough walking through the snow crust herself; but then the old man had collapsed, and she had carried him on her back the last quarter mile. Finally, as the forest thinned, the old man grunted, pointing to a cluster of domes flanked by a pair of chimneys that vented clouds of steam into the diminishing snow squalls.

"That's it," the old man said. "Only a little farther."

"All right. Just let me rest a bit."

"We've got to work, girl! Rest later."

Fortunately, winds had swept most of the snow from this open meadow, and the old man was able to walk most of the rest of the way to the station. When they reached three huge pipelines feeding into the power-houses, he put his hands on one and nodded with satisfaction.

"Still running. This is steam heated in the collectors up on the surface."

"We saw them when we came in. Only half the grid was working."

"Nobody to maintain it. Same thing with the Dragonsback."

"Dragonsback?"

"The mirrors. All wrecked by now, I suppose."

"Some of them were still standing."

"Mmm. These lines, after the steam condenses, take the water down to the lake. Comes back up as vapor. The intakes for the condensers are three terraces above this level. More than likely, that's how the ice roof got its start." He spat in the snow. "There's a service bay here. Let's find the door."

A quarter of the way around the first dome the old man stopped and put his hand on a red circle, the only mark on an otherwise perfect glass wall. He swore sharply when nothing happened; then he rubbed his hands together briskly and tried again. Whatever machinery the circle was supposed to activate failed to respond.

"What's wrong?"

"Locked or frozen. I'm not sure." For the first time the old man's glittering eyes seemed to dull. "Perhaps we should try the City."

"The city down there is buried under tons of ice. This place still works. I think I can open the door, if you don't mind another 'trick.' "

The old man thought about it. "Concentrate only on the door," he finally said. "Because if you don't, I'll knock you on the head!" He picked up a good-sized chunk of ice to show he meant it.

"Only on the door."

Katya stepped up to the wall and began concentrating on the red circle. Soon her inner vision let her pass through the wall and examine the locking mechanism. Moving closer, she found the dark chip of circuitry that controlled the palm switch. Condensation inside the wall had ruined it long ago; consequently, there was no magnetic beam to trip the doorway motors, which seemed in good condition.

Katya provided the beam herself. Far away she heard the door groaning in its tracks, and the old man impatiently urging her to finish.

But she did not want to finish. She was certain about the door opening now, so she bolted, soaring out in search of her brother. She felt free and powerful —nothing can hurt me!—as she opened her mind and called to him.

Jes?

Silence. Then: *Not now, damn you, I'm*—

She heard the proximity alarms on the flight deck of Morgan's ship. She saw the main screen alive with the blips of dart-shaped fighter craft that matched every evasive maneuver he tried. They were going to bring him down.

Let me help you!

Katya sensed weapons fire. No time to wait for his permission. She expanded out of the flight deck, spreading herself like an umbrella between the ship and the sensors of the pursuit fleet. Turning away, she threw back a false image into their navigation equipment, while Jes sought cover in the tremendous waterfall spouting from the hole in the ice cap. He looped around, out of range, while Katya lingered in the spray an instant longer.

The six dart ships hit the vault at full power and exploded with a concussion that rocked every terrace in the canyon.

Okay, Jes, they're gone. Now please come back for me. I'm at a power station—

No answer. Something cut the connection the way it had been cut on Morgan. Katya shuddered and tried to pull away. She found she couldn't move.

He will come to me. A voice, soft and sweet as the voice of a child, held her. *But you can have him back,* the voice went on, *in return for your help.*

Why? Why do you need me?

Because of this. And the voice showed her the silent place in the heart of the galaxy. It was a graveyard, where the shades of the frozen dead wheeled by, faintly reflecting the single spark her own life provided.

This fate is the fate of all Minds like ours, child. Help me. Help me.

The dark heart of the Cold turned toward her. It began to open like a flower of darkness, and Katya felt the emptiness begin to seize her own heart. She tried to pull away, but it was strong, and she had nothing to anchor herself with, nothing to hold.

Then came an explosion of pain, and it was light that settled around her after all.

CHAPTER 16

"These are craws?"

First Speaker Rowen held out a wriggling crustacean by its shell and smiled. Janoo had just brought up a whole net full of them from the sea.

"We called them crayfish. One of my favorite things to eat."

The boy said nothing, dumping the catch into a steaming glass cooking pot. Janoo had found the pot, and the wood for the fire beneath it, after Rowen and the boy set up camp along a catwalk beneath the edge of Terrace 3-C.

They had walked a long time to reach this spot. Now that the Speaker had a chance to sit, the shock of his transformation—the world's transformation—was finally beginning to sink into him. All he had to do was look beyond the edge of the terrace to understand: half the world a desert, the sea shrunken and populated with mutants like this boy, the whole canyon darkened under a shield of ice. And Weiring, his fishing city, the place of his honorable retirement, was buried in red sand.

And this had all happened for Rowen in an instant. He had embraced the suspension block. Then he turned around to stare at a boy in a Technician's uniform. No time between for Conteirre to suffer such disaster, and yet time *had* passed. According to Janoo, almost nineteen hundred years of time. Time for the sand, the ice, and the frozen sea. Time for Sinom to win.

This was as close to a despairing moment as Rowen had even had. Janoo sensed it, and came over with a shelled craw, touching it gently to Rowen's mouth. He forced himself to chew it. Somehow the fact that the rich, snowy meat tasted the same as ever reassured him. He felt better.

Rav tossed away an empty shell and unfastened the front of his suit. Letting it fall to his waist, he tilted the water jug and poured a stream over his face. The muscles of his powerful chest contracted; spray blew from the gill slits under his arms. He stretched, refitted the suit, then sat solemnly again.

"Must you do that often?" Rowen asked.

Rav shrugged. "I don't know. This is the longest I've ever been out of the sea."

"The rest of your people—do they spend all their time in the water?"

"All but a few like me who are said to be air breathers." Rav's voice was bitter. "Those whom the world has no use for." He watched Rowen take the jug and drink. He said, "And when do you breathe water, sky god?"

"I can't." Rowen smiled. "My people lost that ability hundreds of millions of years ago. Yours have received the gift again."

"It's a curse!" The boy showed emotion for the first time. "The sea is our prison, the Mother's farm. We're to eat and grow fat and breed until the hunter ships come to take us away." He made an emphatic sign, jabbing both hands downward away from the fire before lapsing into sullen silence. Rowen waited for Janoo to open another crayfish before speaking again.

"Rav, Janoo tells me that the ships you speak of, the hunter ships, take youngsters to . . . Heaven . . . to be with the Mother. To become part of what she is. Don't the people consider this to be a great honor?"

"Some do. Those that believe the old, frightened teachers."

"What do your teachers say?"

"Don't you know? Didn't the sky gods create the Mother?"

Janoo buzzed and landed in Rowen's lap, purring as Rowen stroked the shell between his eye stalks. "We were not gods, Rav, but yes, we did help create her. Once she was a woman, like your Luci, but . . . different, with special abilities to hear and see things that others could not. She wanted all of us to become like her." And she's won, he thought.

Rav nodded. "We are told that the sea is only a beginning place for us. The people are like fingerlings—undeveloped animals which grow into something more. When children reach my age, there's a ceremony: The Mother's priestess chooses those who will stay to care for the children, to be mothers and fathers and work to build things and catch food for the rest. Those who are not chosen are taken by the ships to a place where the Mother cares for them. They leave their bodies while the mind is taken by her to nourish her and keep her strong."

"Do your teachers give you a reason for this."

"Reason? I don't understand you."

"Do they tell you why the Mother takes children? Why she stays *here,* rather than leaving the world and traveling as we—as the sky gods—once did?"

"They say the Mother is not yet strong enough. That outside Heaven is a place that is dark and cold—that would swallow her up and all of us with her. The priestess explained that there were not enough minds within the Mother for her to be able to escape. It is because of the sea people being too weak, or so they say. So they must have more. Every harvest the take is younger, and our people grow fewer. We must submit. The Mother punishes those territories that resist."

"And you believe all these things?"

The boy's eyes flashed. "Do I believe in the Mother? I've seen the sea desert where black water ran from the

Palisades veins and killed thousands of sea people. Do
I believe in the sky gods?'' He pulled a thong around
his neck and exposed a worn coin—Citizens' currency.
''These are everywhere, as are the wrecks of your flying
machines. I myself saw a piece of metal transformed
into a living being. So to say I don't believe would be the
words of a fool. But I do not accept this! My teachers
would have had me surrender to the hunters because
that is what has always been done. But something here''
—he tapped his forehead—''tells me, Rav, it does not
make sense for beautiful people to be born into the
world only to be taken away. Mothers and teachers and
crècheholders live to get old, and I see the sadness on
their faces when their children are taken from them. If
the Mother truly loved us, she would not permit such
sadness to exist. And if she were truly good, wouldn't
she be able to prevail against the devils who built this
world? How can the Mother know better than they,
when she is confined here and they roam freely? No. My
heart tells me it is wrong.''

"Were you prepared to fight then, Rav?"

Rav snorted. ''There are big fish and little fish. The
little fish I'm able to eat because I can catch them; I
hide from the big fish. Luci and I were going to start
something different. We will yet, when I reach the city
and take her back.'' He looked at Rowen defiantly. ''Or
will you try to stop me?''

"Why would I want to stop you?"

''The Mother is your creature. The Father wishes to
protect his Daughter.''

''True enough. But this world is my daughter, Rav,
and it hurts me very much to see it as it is now. Once—
only a moment ago for me—Conteirre was alive with
happy people on every terrace. There were no deserts,
and the sea was twice as big as it is now. The Mother
was nothing but an old woman with a small band of
followers. Our future was bright. It was my hope to see
the transformation of this whole planet into a world as
green as those few terraces you want to reach. But
something happened. Somehow the people lost sight of

what they truly wanted and chose the Mother's way.
And now my world is nearly dead. I won't try to stop
you, Rav. I'll do anything I can to help save what's left.
Fortunately we have Janoo to help us, but we'll need
more—"

Rav cut him off. "If the Mother is unable to change
her world, how can we think of changing ours? I only
want Luci."

"But your duty—"

"My duty was to allow myself to be pulled into a
hunter ship, sky god! I refused. My duty is to myself!"

Abruptly he went off a little way, smoothed some
sand, and lay down, knees drawn up, with his arms for a
pillow. He was still and soon Rowen heard the deep,
troubled breathing of someone forcing himself to sleep.
How hard it must be for him, Rowen thought. And how
hard for me.

Distant thunder from an upper-level storm rumbled
through the canyon as soft lightning flashes made the
dune tops dance. The world was still alive, but what of
the Citizenry? Surely there were others beside the water
breathers harvested for incorporation in Sinom's group
consciousness. Sky gods, hunters . . . what was their
relationship to the Mother? Could they perceive, as Rav
did, Sinom's failure and the impending doom that faced
the ecosystems and, if Rav's myths had any basis in
reality, the Mind itself?

The Citizenry in mortal danger again. Rowen considered what facts he knew, and as he did he felt the old
excitement, the challenge, of leadership returning. You
are First Speaker. You helped make this world a safe
haven for the children of the Exodus. And you must
fight—even as this sea child wanted to fight—to save it
now. Any way you can.

Rowen stood, brushing sand from his suit. When he
chirped softly, Janoo buzzed from somewhere behind
him and landed on his shoulder. Its eye stalks popped
up and waved inquisitively.

"Yes, little one, we work together again. I want you
to go to the other side and make a survey. Find what ter-

races are still productive, what machinery still works, where the settlements are now. And a floater that works, if you can manage to tie into the controls. Tomorrow we'll be traveling up Terraces Four and Five. Meet us on the way."

The Xein buzzed, retracted its claws, and spun away into the dusky canyon night.

"Find me Citizens I can lead," Rowen murmured after it.

CHAPTER 17

The fire had gone down and Janoo still had not returned when Rowen was awakened roughly by the sea boy. He sat up, watched dew beads make tracks down the front of his suit, rubbed his eyes. Then he remembered where he was.

Somehow sleep had given him the weight of some of those missing centuries, and Rowen suddenly felt brittle, ready to crack under the pressure of time. A few yards away, Rav pissed over the catwalk rail without a trace of self-consciousness, moving his lean, streamlined body with easy grace. When Rowen got up to do likewise, he found it necessary to turn away.

"There's craws left," Rav said when Rowen came back.

"It's not my habit to eat in the morning. I'll take some."

"The flesh won't keep." Rav turned the cooking pot over the side of the catwalk. Then he noticed Rowen staring out over the expanse between the terrace edge and the opposite side of the canyon.

"Where's your familiar, sky god?"

"On his way back, I hope. I sent him to have a look at the terraces across the bridge."

"Why? We'll be there soon enough." Rav tied the net with the water jug inside a loop that he slung over his shoulder. Then he looked down at Rowen. "Ready?"

"I think we should wait for the Xein."

"I thought you had a crusade to begin."

"If you want to call it that. I think of it as a simple journey. But whatever it is, we should not undertake it without adequate information . . ." He broke off as he noticed how the boy was smiling at him.

"You're afraid of the climb, aren't you?"

"Certainly not!"

Rav began laughing. "I watched you all yesterday. You took every step as though it was your last one. You don't want to look down, but you can't help yourself either. Ho!"

"It's not funny. I took a fall when I was a child, from a cliff—" Why am I trying to justify myself to him?

"A sky god, afraid of heights!" Rav gasped, wiping his eyes. "You'll pardon me, but the idea—the mystery and fear we felt about you, and you're afraid of heights!"

Rowen turned red. "You don't know what it means to fall, do you?" He pushed Rav back toward the railing. "You've spent your life floating." Another push. "Cushioned. Let me tell you what it's like, Rav—flying. Only at the end—"

"I know, I know!" Rav glanced down at the rippled dunes in the terrace below. "I fell . . . from the hunter ship." He looked embarrassed suddenly.

"Then you can appreciate that it's rather difficult for me here."

For a moment, neither one spoke. Then Rav said, "But the crab won't be able to carry you to the other side."

"True."

"So we must use the bridge. And to get to it, we have to climb."

Rowen sighed. "Very well. But we have no rope."

"We have this." He took the bottle net from his shoulder and unknotted the cord with practiced fingers. "It's very strong. Feel." Rowen tugged uncertainly at it. He'd never be able to pull it apart, but that didn't mean it could support anyone's full weight. "It's all we have, sky god. Here, knot it around your waist. I'll lead the way. I've stared up many times at the rocks below that bridge—and they're run through with cracks and places where the stone has fallen away. It's not more than three hundred feet, with many handholds and ledges to rest on. Drink this water, sky god, and get ready."

Rowen nodded. This was his test, and if he failed now he was no longer worthy to lead his people. He tilted the bottle back and rinsed his mouth. Rav then broke it against the metal deck, saving the jagged neck, which he wound tightly with cord.

"We may need this to wedge inside cracks," he explained. "Come on."

The catwalk ended in a narrow ledge that followed the bottom of the terrace face. The facing was made of concrete—Rowen recalled approving the contracts to have the work done. Staring up at this massive wall that seemed to reach all the way to the sky, he wished he had not. Before, the facings had been webbed glass girders, probably much easier to scale.

"Here, we're in luck already." Rav pointed to a service ladder a few yards to the north, one that led to a tiny platform jutting out of the face. "That's half our journey right there." He ran up to it—Rowen having no choice but to follow when the cord stretched tight—and started climbing with incredible agility. Halfway up he stopped. "Sky god!"

"Very well." Rowen took hold of the first rung, but the spun-fiber rod seemed too slippery to grip.

"Don't think of it as climbing. Imagine you're crawling over this ladder on the ground. You're going forward, not up."

You can't let her win! he thought. Slowly he took the first few steps. There wasn't much clearance between the ladder and the concrete, and he was forced to climb with knees and elbows out. When Rav was satisfied that Rowen was moving properly, he took the rest of the ladder and pulled himself onto the platform. He sat there swinging his legs, staring at the awesome panorama of sea and ice-sky merging in two sweeping curves.

"I always thought Alissia was so big. But it's nothing!"

Rowen hooked his arms around the rails and looked up. "There's not room for both of us on that platform. Keep going."

"Which way looks most promising to you?"

He's toying with me, Rowen thought. "To the right. That fracture runs all the way to the top."

"But there's a ledge to get over as well."

"Go to the right!"

"Yes, sky god, to the right! Only remember it was your idea." He reached over his head, found a good handhold, and lifted himself off the platform. This time he climbed more slowly, so that Rowen was able to catch his breath on the platform before the rope around his waist pulled tight again.

Imagine you're crawling. Rowen tried, but with the super-structure of the bridge set against the green of the ice vault like ivory bones washed on the shore of a silent sea, it was difficult. He kept wanting to follow the bridge with his eyes, even though he knew he must watch where Rav placed his hands and feet. He remembered the heroic efforts that had gone into the construction of that bridge, how in a single accident twenty-three workers had plunged through a faulty safety net to their deaths after a scaffold cable had snapped. The bridge had been christened in their honor: Work Brigade Sixteen Bridge, and Rowen had dedicated the commemorative plaque himself. Had it been worth so much just to build such a symbol when no one remembered what had been sacrificed to throw it across the terraces?

If it helps me succeed, yes! Rowen's fingers ached; the heavy cold downdrafts from the turbulent clouds hugging the upper east-side terraces threatened to tear him from the wall. Maybe Sinom herself knew he was

coming and was ready to flick him away like a troublesome insect. Alone, I'm nothing, but on the other side
. . . Rowen heard the whip-song of cord whirling
through the air; he looked up and saw that Rav had
wedged himself between jutting blocks and was trying to
throw his bottle up over the ledge. Twice he failed, but
the third time it snagged, jamming tight when the boy
yanked on the line. Rav took care not to rely on it
totally, more or less vaulting up and over the obstacle.

He looked over the edge. "You can walk it from here,
sky god. Do you want me to pull you the rest of the
way?"

"Don't trust the rope," Rowen gasped. His lungs
were flaming on either side of his hammering heart.

"You're going to have to swing your leg up. Give me
your hand."

"I can't . . . reach."

"Sky god, you have to."

"A moment." He shifted his position to gain a better
reach. Rav's webbed fingers locked on his own.

"That's it. Now get ready."

Rowen closed his eyes, tensed his muscles, and
kicked. His heel slammed into the top of the ledge but
landed on loose pebbles. For a moment he fought the
slide—then lost, falling back. He heard Rav's surprised
yelp as their fingers parted and he began to drop.

The cord dug into his waist. He opened his eyes and
realized he was dangling ten feet below the shelf.

"Rav!"

The boy looked down at him, grinning with real
pleasure. "What did I tell you about my cord? You
didn't even have time to scream." Then, seemingly
without effort, he pulled Rowen the rest of the way up.

The roadway of the ancient bridge was torn to rubble
in places, but the span itself remained sound, and the
two of them found the crossing easy. Just beyond the
halfway point, at the apex of the gentle, thrusting arch,
they found water collected in depressions on the deck.

Rowen stopped to drink, Rav to breathe water in and blow out his dessicated water lungs.

Rowen sat down to rest, listening to the distant sound of thunder rumbling down from the heights. Watching the scudding clouds momentarily clear away from the ice vault, he shook his head. "How can that exist?"

"The sky's the sky," Rav said, examining the soles of his feet.

"No. In my day we had a real sky, open to space. Sometimes when all the lights were off in the terraces you could see right into the heart of it. Thousands and thousands of stars."

"Stars?"

"Points of light in the sky. Each one of them is a ball of fire thousands of times the size of this world. Some of them have worlds of their own circling around them, and some of those have people on them. People who have never heard of the Mother."

Rav shrugged. "I don't care about such things. Why should I? There's no way to travel to such places." He stood up. "Anyway, we have enough problems. Let's go."

Rowen tried to stand, but his legs had stiffened in the short time he'd been sitting. He rolled forward, groaning like an old man, then looked up to see Rav staring at him disgustedly, hands on his hips.

"You are a poor example of a god," he said before helping Rowen to his feet. Somehow Rowen found that incredibly funny, and it was some time before he stopped laughing long enough to begin walking again.

The sharp evening shadow nearly reached the end of the bridge by the time Rowen and the boy finally reached the cool, fragrant margin of Terrace 4C. Seeing pastureland and crops that were still being tended restored some of Rowen's shattered confidence. Crops meant people—Citizens whom he could mold into an effective force to resist Sinom and her composite Mind. He was back in his element now, back in a part of Conteirre which even two thousand years had not begun to change. He hopped off the roadway onto thick green turf. A sharp breeze brought crackling thunder and the smell of ozone heralding an evening storm. Rav's strength had flagged badly during the last part of the crossing, but he had refused all offers that they stop and rest for a while. Now even his determination was no longer enough to drive him. He sat in the grass with knees drawn close to his body, heedless of the rain that spattered his back.

"Rav, there are some buildings over there." He pulled the boy up. "Come on. You'll get sick this way, and pneumonia's something I can't treat."

This is better, he thought, guiding his shivering companion. The way it should be. He's nothing without the physical superiority. The rain chased them along the path leading to a gated fence. Rowen opened it and hustled Rav inside the closest building, a domed structure smelling of fresh-cut fodder. Rain rattled the triangular panels, but it was warm and dry inside. All he lacked was light—and food. His concern for Janoo's whereabouts sprang up again, but he told himself the Xein would return, probably during the night. Perhaps he took my orders too literally. But malfunction was a real possibility as well, though Rowen resisted the thought. Any machine could fail after so many years.

"We've done well today, Rav. Tomorrow we'll see what sort of Citizens tend these farms."

Rav lay down. "That doesn't matter to me." He closed his eyes, and Rowen saw that he had fallen asleep.

He smiled, tired from the long trek himself. There would be more ground to cover tomorrow, but he was looking forward to the challenge. Life had been offered him again; this time, Rowen had no intention of foolishly throwing it away.

He dozed until the spotlights assailed his eyes; until strong, rough hands pulled him to his feet. At first he could not understand the speech of the people training their lights—and weapons—on him. But then—

". . . uniforms. They have to be from Meems."

Rowen extended his palms in a gesture of peace. "Citizens," he began. A heavy woman with iron-gray hair stepped to the front of the group.

"Citizens, is it? I'll show you Citizens, pig!"

Too late Rowen saw the sweep of an ax handle before the world exploded into crackling streaks of red.

CHAPTER 18

The purple fur coat was spread out on the floor, with Katya lying on top of it. Gradually she became aware of the fact that her nose itched. She sneezed loudly, and when she did, the fierce-looking old man came over with a cup of steaming liquid in his hands. He approached cautiously, kneeling beside her, saying nothing until Katya blinked her eyes open.

"Still here, girl?"

She tried to sit up—too quickly. Gods, I'm taking a pounding this trip! she thought. Then she realized that the old man had hit her.

"Get your hands off me!"

"That's more like it," he said. "I was afraid I'd used a little too much force."

Katya rubbed her eyes and tried to make the dizziness go away. She'd been in touch with Jesse, until . . .

"Where are we?"

"The power station. You succeeded in opening the doorway, but unfortunately did not listen to my warning. You were going under. Sinom let you have a taste of the Cold—an old trick of hers. She'll put you into it, and wait until you're just about lost, and then offer to save you. For a price. In your case, a considerable one."

"What are you talking about, old man?"

"My name is Tyron. Be grateful for that bump on your head. For the sake of that useless brother of yours, you would have surrendered to Sinom. On her terms. Without a fight. I couldn't let that happen. You're safe, as long as you listen to me. Now, I've found rations, and we'll be warm and safe here. We can prepare. We—"

He stopped. His mouth opened. When Katya entered his mind the soup cup crashed to the floor. *All right, old man, I want answers. I want everything in that old husk of yours, and I want it now.*

It was a brutal, humiliating journey through Tyron's memory. Katya took satisfaction from his shame, pushed past it, past the terror of the long age he'd spent as a mind-ravaged prisoner in his cell, until she could see this world—Conteirre—as Tyron had known it. Lush farmlands. Hanging gardens. Rainbows arcing across the chasm from one terrace to another. Conteirre City with its emerald towers and the cavernous Diet of Citizens, where political struggles over the future of the Citizenry were waged and lost. First Speaker Rowen's inexplicable disappearance. The blond-haired Gaelen's assumption of power and the first huge construction projects near Meems. Ten thousand cells, then fifty thousand, and a hundred thousand after that. Conteirre in the grip of a fever; Gaelen speaking to half a million Citizens on Terrace 4, with Lady Sinom shrouded in white beside him, surveying the crowd impassively with her one good eye, reaching out to it through Gaelen, pouring her dreams of immortality, evolution beyond biology, beyond divinity.

And Katya saw the lie behind it, the pride that made Sinom believe she could escape the fate of the aborigines . . . escape the Cold . . . the trap.

Tyron knew that trap. Back toward the terror . . . Rowen's final visit to examine the archaeological site. Rowen must not think of resigning! The challenge will keep him, certainty about that, some pride in being able to maneuver the First Speaker so easily, fear of Sinom.

Always suspected that the Lady had found this world to carry out her plans, that somehow Sinom might even have caused the nova that destroyed the homeworld. But Sinom would lose.

A good dinner, a drink from the bottle of 150-year-old brandy, part of the family stock, all burned up but these few precious drops. Growing grapes now on Terraces 17 and 23, but winemaking was still a Class 3 agricultural priority. By stars, we'll have to get the First Speaker to change that soon. Noise in the front of the cabin. Cowled men enter the house, Committee men from the look of them, perhaps mindlinked as well. Want to make an example of me. "See? Tyron's among the first to enter the Mind. He's cast his voice in favor of the Committee's program." Can't let them do it. Shoot me instead, murder me and they'll see what good propaganda *that* makes. Out the back, tempt them. They're coming, but confused, the relaying of orders is too slow, and they're incapable of making decisions on their own when linked that way to Lady Sinom. Old bird! Catch me if you can! In the trench now, caught my heel on a rebar, falling toward the stones. Dare her. Dare her to take me now.

"Want me, old woman?"

Touches the black stones. Both of them. Drowning. No air, no light, just emptiness where the voices of the desperate Lost waft through like currents of hydrogen in deepest space. A thread. Lizard faces, aborigines sense me, realize I'm a link to their home, gathering like metal dust around a lodestone. The loneliness, the anger, the frustration of ages of imprisonment, all in their voices, millions of them, begging for freedom, wanting to escape through me, escape through me, escape through—

Katya broke contact. Shaking, she put her hands over her face and wept. Tyron recovered after a moment, sighed, put his arm around her.

"I could have told you all of it," he said gently.

"I know. I'm sorry." She was so frightened, angry at herself and at Jes, angry at how the worlds everywhere had always rejected both of them. "Oh, Tyron, what is it?" she said.

He brought her another cup of soup. The fierceness had left him, and he looked troubled as he spoke.

"When I touched the stones, and they came to me all at once, I lost my reason, my awareness. I remember things . . . but they make no sense—or didn't, until you rescued me. You gave me my mind back, Katya. For that, I owe you my life. Is the soup too hot?"

"It's just fine." She tried to smile.

"That's better. What I'm trying to say is, I can only tell you theories I'd half developed before the Mind of the aborigines tried to save itself through me. First, you must answer a question. Did you ever sense that anything like the Cold existed?"

"No."

Tyron nodded. "Neither did Sinom. And the aboriginal priests who built this canyon into a shrine for their sect didn't suspect it either. But I can say that the Cold is a thing that consumes minds. Not small minds of limited power, such as I or your brother or even you alone possess. But larger minds. Minds that pose a threat to an orderly universe. Minds like the one Sinom controls. The Cold grabbed the Citizenry as soon as enough of us were mindlinked for it to notice. And only the strength of that old woman's will has kept most of the people resting safely in their cells. She has strength enough to hang on here, just as the aborigines have, with their sacred stones."

"They're anchors, you mean?"

"Of a sort. But Sinom is losing her grip. The fact that I could call to you for help in the midst of my madness proves she no longer has power to control the canyon as she did before. She may soon be swept into the void, and the Citizenry along with it. The universe will be safe again from powers like Sinom, who might wish to roam free and contest with other powers for control of material worlds. Rogue gods, immature, full of themselves, battling for preeminence. Creation could not stand against such chaos, girl. That's why the Cold exists. The

Cold is an immunological reaction to the disease of great power. Minds without anchors to a physical world, such as Sinom is fortunate enough to have right now, are caught up by the Cold, which sucks life utterly into the void. Without mercy. It possesses no consciousness itself, hence no morality, no remorse. It simply does. And as far as I can know, no Mind has ever defeated it."

"But Sinom—this groupmind—might, if I help her?"

"It's a question of strength. The attraction of the Cold is like that of a whirlpool—a powerful, irresistible current. Sinom's problem has been that she cannot focus the entire Mind on pulling away. There is a limit to how many cells she can use at once, and she must aways employ a good deal of her capacity keeping life-support systems and energy and food systems operating. She believes that if you take part of the burden, she'll be able to concentrate on the final struggle. That's why she called you here. That's why she's separated you from your brother. She'll swallow him up, then entice you with the prospect of getting him back."

He fell silent as Katya finished her soup. Then he said, "You see there's no way for you to leave Conteirre without meeting her. And fighting your way out."

"I don't see that. I don't know if I believe in your Cold. And I certainly don't believe that a pair of stones is all that's saving the groupmind from destruction. If Sinom is weakening, as you say, why not simply wait? She'll die, and Conteirre will be free."

Eyes flashing, he said, "When the Cold takes her, it will also take the occupants of over two million life-support cells. I want to destroy the old woman *and* save those lives. You can help me do that."

"How?"

"Wait. Allow Sinom to offer her bait—"

"My brother, you mean?"

"Yes."

"Forget it, Tyron!"

"Perhaps," he said, "you didn't understand. There's no other way."

"I want my brother back. That's all I care about. We came here by accident, and as far as I'm concerned, your problems are none of my business."

"Stop fooling yourself, girl!"

"I'm not." The place Tyron had taken her to was part of a service bay. Among the scattered machine parts and crumbling vehicles, Katya spotted an open disk-shaped craft that looked like it might be able to fly. Pointing to it, she said, "Is that thing capable of taking us to the other side?"

"It's charging right now," Tyron said.

"I want you to take me to Jes."

"You would certainly lose both your brother and your life."

"I'll take my chances. Now will you guide me? Or will I have to find out what I want to know from you— the hard way?"

"Force has a certain attraction, does it not?"

"Tyron!"

"I will take you closer in return for a promise of caution. You need my knowledge of the foe, Katya. You need me."

She stared at him, felt the lump he'd raised on the top of her head. Maybe he *had* saved her. And it wouldn't do to go rushing into Sinom's territory without knowing what she was facing. That was Jes's way. Finally, in spite of everything, she smiled a little.

"Before all this happened, Tyron, you weren't by any chance known for being stubborn, were you?"

"Fortunately," he said, "I can't remember."

Once charged, the flying craft—Tyron called it a floater—seemed to work well enough. It took them skimming over the ground until the terrace fell away, leaving them with nothing but fifteen miles of turbulent air between themselves and the pewter-colored sea. For the first time Katya saw the tremendous scope of the canyon. They had landed on the side that was to all appearances dead: ice at the upper levels, red desert below. Tyron explained that the ice vault was responsi-

ble for a circular movement of the atmosphere, which
rose along the west wall, warm and moisture-laden,
moving toward the cooler middle terraces to deposit
rain. By the time it reached the ice vault and began to
fall along the eastern terraces, and thus compress and
heat up, all the rain had been wrung out of it.

Katya clutched a grab bar in front of her seat as an
updraft drove them up and just as violently released
them. Tyron seemed unconcerned, however, and she
forced herself to concentrate on the landscape of the
lush terrace immediately ahead.

"Are those animals on those hillsides?"

"Milchers. This is still dairyland. We didn't bring
many other animals from the homeworld. That ought to
be Terrace Seventeen. Two below the Work Brigade
Bridge. Hidden in the clouds somewhere down there—"

The floater bucked suddenly, losing power.

"What's wrong?"

"If I had the tools and the time, girl, maybe I could
tell you! Hold on!" Tyron pulled the floater's nose up
and gave it as much power as he could. It was a struggle
to gain a few hundred feet of altitude, and the lip of the
closest terrace seemed impossibly far away, but somehow Tyron found some lift and glided over to the safety
of green grass just as the motors quit altogether. Once
they were down and he was satisfied that Katya had suffered no injury—touching, she thought, considering
how he'd used that chunk of ice on her before—he tried
to restart the floater. Unfortunately, it refused to work.

"Want me to try?"

"No. There're freight lifts at the top of this terrace.
Walking there will give us time to think." He kicked the
side of the floater as he said this, his leg making the
front of the purple fur coat flap comically. Then they
started off. After a rather pleasant walk through pastureland, they reached a grove of rubbery-looking
trees whose big-lobed, yellow-green leaves bore fruit along
their edges. Tyron tore some off and handed her one.
When Katya bit it hesitantly, bright purple juice
ran down her chin. The taste was something like a cran-

berry mixed with sweet lime. Strange, but not at all unpleasant.

"These are still the same, at least," Tyron said. "Fill your pockets. No telling when we'll find something else to eat."

Katya did, using the big leaves for wrappers. They walked on as the slope gradually increased. They passed beneath the edge of the next terrace up, and into a different, paler light radiating from its support superstructure. Here the grass changed as well, becoming thicker, wider-bladed, almost blue. Katya noticed that the grazing milchers seemed to prefer the pastures grown under the artificial lighting. Fortunate for them, and for the meat eaters of this world.

Suddenly Tyron stopped, cocking his head into the wind.

"What's wrong?"

"Shh! Can't you hear that? It's not possible!"

"What's not possible? Tyron?" She braced herself for another shock. Meanwhile, Tyron put his fingers to his mouth and whistled sharply three times.

A moment later something small and dark flew straight at them. Katya yelped and threw herself to the ground as the thing buzzed over her head. It was on Tyron! She rolled over and got ready to use her mind to help him, and then realized that he wasn't struggling with an attacker. Instead he hugged the thing. It looked like a cross between a crab and a hubcap, and it responded to the old man's caresses with a deep metallic purr.

"What in the world is that?" Katya got up just as the thing snapped its button eyes around toward her on their flexible stalks.

"This is Janoo. It's a Xein—the only living things we found in this canyon when we arrived from the homeworld. Normally lives in the shallows up near Northend, but, for Rowen, I made a few improvements: sensors, flight propulsion, extra capacity in the brain. This was his bodyguard and personal assistant once." Tyron's eyes shone. "Why don't you get out a fig, girl? Make friends."

Cautiously, Katya held out one of the pods. The Xein buzzed twice, then hopped over and landed on her arm. It snatched the fig, flew straight up, and returned to Tyron, this time perching on the old man's head.

"See? A friend. Her name is Katya." Janoo chattered at him, and he nodded. "That's right. An off-worlder. She's going to help us put the old woman in her place. How? Scan her, you miserable beetle!"

Janoo clicked its eyes together and whistled. "Exactly," Tyron chuckled. "Exactly."

"You understand it?"

Tyron touched the skin behind his ears. "Up here there's a bit of circuitry. Still working. Only two other people besides me had the ability: Rowen, and his wife Mehga."

He halted then, and Katya saw something soften the hard lines of his face. Tears pooled in his eyes.

"It can't be true," he whispered.

"What?"

"Janoo. He says that Rowen is alive, and traveling with a companion on the Work Brigade Bridge. Janoo! Listen to me. Go back to him now. Tell him where we are, bring him to us. We'll go to Meems together. We'll free the Citizenry. Now fly!"

But the Xein did not move. It buzzed stubbornly, gripping Tyron's iron-colored hair, until the old man grudgingly handed up six or seven figs.

Then, with a sharp click, it flew off toward the canyon and the bridge that looked finer than spider's silk, strung between a break in the clouds.

Book Five

THE FREE ZONE

CHAPTER 19

The hot lights made Luci's already dry skin feel as though it was on fire. Unkind hands—belonging to whom? they couldn't possibly be the hands of the Mother's servants, or of sky gods; the faces of the women who attended her were narrow and cruel—turned her this way and that on a swiveling stool. Her face had been powdered white. Now they painted vivid red lines about her eyes, filled in her lips with greasy cream that fluoresced the way the stripes of a deep-water tetra did. They had bound her hair so tightly that her head ached, fastening it with pins pushed savagely against her scalp; they had cinched a corset around her waist, yanking it closed until she could scarcely breathe through her raw throat. The appliance pushed her breasts up and in; now they were scratched where one of the harridans had shoved the thorny stem of a yellow flower between them.

"That's what I call dressed fish," one of them said, examining her work. "Ought to keep him busy a minute or two getting through all of this."

Luci had been afraid to speak before, but her thirst and weakness reduced her inhibition. Heaven or not, she needed moisture, and she reached for the bowl of it

135

they'd used to help set her hair.

"*Fresh* fish," another said, snatching it away.

"Please." Her voice was little more than a croak. "I've got to have some water."

"What, and spoil your pretty makeup? Not likely, froggy, not likely. The First Speaker's got to have his look at you first. Save your beggin' for him." With that they pulled her roughly out of the mirrored room, through a corridor that was mercifully cooler, then into a dark room that smelled of moisture and was alive with the sound of running water. As Luci's eyes adjusted, she realized there was a pool in the center of the room, surrounded by lush potted plants, its surface dotted with floating blossoms. She strained toward it—and felt something cold and hard clamp around her ankle. Then the door shut on her escorts' laughter as they left her alone.

She was only a step away from the water, but it was a step she could not take. The chain binding her legs wasn't long enough. Suddenly the despair she had been fending off ever since she had been taken from Rav and packed into the hold of the hunter ship finally overcame her, and she sank to the stone floor. What sort of gods were these? The pain and the fear were bad enough, but even worse was her inability to understand what was happening to her. Where was the Mother, now that she had been taken to Heaven? Where was the blissful union her teachers had spoken of so often? Perhaps this was a punishment for her sins, her doubt, the sacrilege of removing her collar and saving Rav with it. But if she deserved punishment, what of the others who had willingly surrendered to the hunters? They had been as cruelly treated as she, unloaded like fish into that crowded tank, only to be snatched away one by one by sky gods and taken away—screaming with pain, some of them—to where? Surely not to the Mother. This had to be a dream.

Let me wake up, Mother. Let me be in my crèche niche still, with Rav waiting for me at the window.

"A vast improvement." Luci turned her head in the

direction of the voice. Standing there was an air breather with the most beautiful face she had ever seen, all crowned with hair like spun gold, bronze-skinned, with eyes of pale, almost gray blue. Surely *this* was a god of the sky, come to save her.

"Thank you, Mother," she whispered aloud.

"What's that?" The man reached down to pick up part of the chain, let some of the slack slide through his fist. "Did I hear you say the word 'Mother'? How very reverent of you, considering what you've been through." Keeping hold of the chain, he sat on a curved bench. "I'm sure she appreciates your faith. Come here. What is your name?"

"Luci." Fighting dizziness, she got up, moving as he wound the chain around his wrist until she was standing unsteadily beside him. There was something wrong with his eyes. They were bloodshot and unfocused, the way those of W'ring men and women got when they drank too much weed spirit.

"Sit down, Luci." He grasped her chin and pulled her face up. "Trembling! Don't you feel well?"

"I've been out of water too long."

"That is a problem. But surely you realize that things have changed for you, Luci. You're in Heaven now. Do you know who I am?"

"One . . . one of the sky gods?"

"A question in your voice! Yes, I am what you say, and more. I am *the* sky god, Luci. And I have chosen you to be with me for a time . . . to provide some comfort to a weary power. Think of it! Of all the ones I could have picked, it's you with me now. And I intend to reward your worthiness, Luci, by pulling you up to my level, by granting you the same immortality I possess, if only for a moment."

He kissed her suddenly, forcing his tongue between her teeth, his fingers gripping her neck in a half stranglehold that left her faint with pain. When he finally released her, the glowing lip cream was smeared across his teeth and upper lip.

"You are sweet, Luci," he breathed, reaching for the

bracelet on her ankle and releasing it. "There's no need for that now. You're not going anywhere." Again he pressed his face against hers, smothering her cry as he pulled the flower from her corset, scratched the stem against the tender skin in back of her arms. Then, one by one, he began loosening the corset stays with his other hand. Luci had been with Rav when he had acted this way, but it had been out of love, with herself an eager participant. Rav had never hurt her, never *taken*, the way this sky god wished to.

Bells rang from the wall behind them. When they did not stop, the sky god swore and pushed Luci away. Not comprehending, she watched as he opened part of the wall, revealing a cube of darkness, faintly shimmering around its perimeter.

"What is it!" The sky god was clearly annoyed.

A woman's voice came from the cube. At the sound of it the god lost some of his anger, his body sagging as if the voice were a great weight on him.

"The boy got through, husband."

"How! I sent my best pilots."

"They would have succeeded, but the sister interfered. He has reached Sinom's compound now." Luci saw something move inside the cube; the sky god grew very pale.

"Surely you can't blame me for that! I did my best. I have my guards, Mehga. I swear I'll fight!"

"Commendable. But the girl and Tyron must still come to Meems. They are traveling from Terrace Seventeen. Elevator Three. You can still redeem yourself."

"I'm busy now—can you delay them somehow?"

"There are no more chances left for you, Gaelen."

"Very well, I'll come." He glanced over his shoulder at Luci. "Just give me a few moments to get organized."

The cube abruptly disappeared. The sky god wiped his lips with the back of his hands, then went to the door. "Remain where you are, girl. I'll be back to finish this." And then he was gone. Luci closed her eyes and began a prayer of thanks, but the words wouldn't come. How could there be a prayer when Rav had been right about everything? The people of W'ring had been bred to be the Mother's victims. And when they refused to resist, they compounded the crimes of these "gods."

But I will resist. For Rav's sake, and my own, and for the sake of all my brothers and sisters left in the sea, I'll do what I can until they kill me. Luci turned toward the pool, unfastened the rest of the stays binding her waist and covering her breathing slits. Then she plunged into the water.

Above her, the residue of paint and powder spread among the flowers like a foul slick of oil.

CHAPTER 20

"All right, Citizen, wake up!"

Cold water splashed on Rowen's face. Sputtering, he struggled against the improvised harness that pinned him to the wall of an animal stall.

"You've no right to treat me this way!" he was finally able to say. "I'm Rowen. First Speaker of the Diet of Citizens!"

"Is that so!" The people gathered at the open end of the stall laughed. "Well, Mr. First Speaker, that's just your bad luck. This is the Free Zone. And we know what to do with Citizens here, don't we?"

More laughter, and murmured, angry agreement. Rowen heard Rav moan. "But we've done you no harm," he said.

"None that we've found yet. That's all we've got to discuss before we throw you over the side with the rest o' the garbage." His tormentor yanked Rowen's straps.

"Now. Why'd they send you here?"

"No one sent me! I'm Rowen . . . suspended since the time before the Mind came to power here . . . born . . . on the homeworld—"

Another yank, the woman grunting with the effort now. "Those legends belong to me. I'm Mechanic on this terrace, and I won't stand for any motherlovin' spies profanin' what's mine!''

"Not legends . . . history. The truth. The Mother's my enemy as well. This boy and I are on our way up from Alissia to fight her. He's escaped from the hunter ships. Ask him."

Now the woman let up on the strap a little. "That's no sea boy. They die without water."

"He can breathe air. Show her, Rav." Rav had already taken the hint, unsealing the front of his suit and wiggling his arms free. As their captors watched, he raised his arms and sprayed what little moisture remained in his water lungs through his rib-cage vents.

"Look at his hands, and the shape of his head," one of the Free Zoners said. Their leader nodded, considering.

"They didn't have a floater?"

"No, Yannika."

"All right. I'll thrash this out at my place. Kip and Ruthel for guard duty. The rest of you can go home. Don't worry, nothing'll be done without my lettin' you know first. Now give me room to work." Despite the curiosity and open hostility of some of the others, the woman's authority went unchallenged, and the crowd filed out of the stable. There was only the woman and two armed men, each of whom was taller than Rowen by a head.

"Get 'em up. We won't carry grown men. Tie their hands and put a leash on 'em." Rowen was yanked to his feet; his head throbbed where the woman had applied her ax handle, but other than that he was unharmed.

"Are you all right, Rav?"

"Only surprised at how little a sky god can do."

"When will you understand that I'm not a god—"

"Shut up, both of you! You'll follow the path through the door here—and don't try anything. Both of these boys can light smoke in your mouth from half mile away with those guns. Let's go."

The storm that had forced Rowen and Rav to take

shelter had passed, though a curtain of mist still lingered out from the terrace edge, along with faint rumblings of distant thunder. Rowen could see that Rav was grateful for the moist air, taking deep breaths of it as he walked ahead on his leash. Indeed, it was clean and fragrant, the same he'd breathed in W'ring just hours—he corrected himself ruefully, feeling the thongs chafing his wrists—just aeons ago. But it was the same air. And there were Citizens here, already part of some sort of local rebellion, Citizens to crystallize around his cause—if he could win over this irascible woman.

"Any sign of that ship, Kippy?"

"No, ma'am. We used the radiation detectors the way you told us to, but all we could get was traces."

"Goin' where?"

"Up toward the Mother's city."

"Damn! That would've been nice to have round here. We'll have to discuss that, Mr. First Speaker—just what you did with that ship of yours. Maybe you can call it back."

A ship? Rowen said. "It isn't ours. We walked here."

"From the Palisades?"

"From the desert," Rav said. "Then over the broken bridge—" He stopped as the reins were pulled tight. Rowen turned to see Ruthel with his weapon shouldered and pointed skyward—and then heard the familiar buzzing noise of a cyborg Xein in flight.

"Don't shoot—" A clout to the small of his back with the ax handle silenced him. Ruthel's arm swung, following the trajectory of the dark disk. When he pressed the trigger a bolt of green seared the air around them. The black disk glowed bright, wobbled, then dropped smoking onto the grass ten yards ahead of them.

"Good shot, boy!" the old woman cackled. Eager to see his kill, Ruthel pulled Rowen to the spot. Please, gods, let it be a bird.

"Oh, Janoo . . ." Rowen fell to his knees, sickened by the pathetic sight of the crippled Xein trying to spin on the wet grass. Half its claws dangled uselessly. Ruthel flipped it over gingerly with his foot. Kip's bolt had blasted away one of the eye stalks.

"Janoo, huh? This belongs to you?"

"It does. It's my remote probe . . . and computer . . . and friend. Two days ago it saved both our lives. And it was returning from . . . it can't tell me now, its voice is gone. I'd sent it out for a look at the terraces." Rowen closed his eyes, trying to sort out the senseless emanations from the wounded Xein. "It might have been a great help to us," he whispered.

The woman scratched her head. "You're cryin'! I've never known a Citizen who'd cry for anything. Kip, put that thing in your sack—careful now. I want to have a look at it in the shop."

"What for?" Rowen was close to losing his temper. "It's machine and animal both, and crazy with pain. Tinkering will only make its suffering worse!"

The woman's eyes flashed. "Tinkerer, am I? Let me have that bag, Ruthel!" When he handed it over, she bent down and gently dumped Janoo onto the ground. Keeping an eye on its sharp claws, she turned it over and probed the underside of its carapace with long, sensitive fingers. She grunted suddenly, pressed in to release a panel.

"That's a weak-exchange battery!" she exclaimed, giving a tiny gold cylinder a half twist and pulling it from Janoo's body. Instantly its writhing ceased. She returned the deactivated Xein to the sack and turned the battery over in her hands. "Like new. You open up some of that junk that's buried up-terrace and you'll find these. Nothing like this has been made in the Slot for two thousand years." She squinted at Rowen. "And you claimed this belonged to you?"

"Obviously it was coming this way."

"You're broken up! All right, Kippy, take the leashes off 'em. I'm inclined to believe they'll behave themselves." Rowen squeezed his hands as the bindings were unwrapped. When they started up again, Ruthel and

Kip cradled their rifles underneath their arms. "By the way. M'name's Yannika. What do you call the fish?"

"His name is Rav. From W'ring." Rowen pronounced it precisely, hoping that Rav was more inclined to regard him as an ally now.

"And you say you came over the bridge!" Yannika hooted, shaking her head. "Don't know if I believe that, but it's a good story. Deserves a meal, don't it, boys? Kippy, you run on ahead and see if you can get something on the table. There's that salt meat and beans left from supper—and shove a pan of biscuits on the coals while you're at it." She tossed Janoo's battery up and caught it. "Your little friend may not know it now, but he's saved both your hides!"

The old woman's home and workshop was a weathered wood-frame dome half buried in a sodded hillside overlooking most of the farms in the so-called Free Zone, as well as a good stretch of the defensive perimeter that Yannika had established to keep the forces of the upper terraces out of her domain. This consisted of a metal fence with a shallow ditch on either side, not at all formidable-looking. The fence began and ended on opposite sides of Yannika's house; Rowen could see air currents shimmering above it, as if the metal were hot. And when a wind-blown leaf was instantly vaporized as it wafted over the mesh, Rowen understood that his captors had more than their isolated location going for their secessionist movement.

"You take the scopes, Ruthel," Yannika ordered when they reached the house. "If I'm wrong about the egghead, I want to know immediately."

"Yes, ma'am!" Ruthel snapped to, opened a cellar door, and disappeared. A few moments later sensor vanes rose from a patch of concrete on the ground. Yannika smiled with obvious pride.

"That boy's always eager to do what he can to help. Not as bright as his brother, but he more'n makes up for it. Well, come in—and careful you don't knock nothin' over."

Rowen discovered when he went through the door
that her request was not an easy one, for every cubic
foot of the dome was crammed with tools and parts
drawers, power lines and air and gas hoses, testing
equipment, computer terminals, and *pieces*—knocked-
down sections of everything from commodes to floaters
that had been manufactured during Rowen's term as
Speaker. A glass partition lined with sagging shelves
divided off the rear third of the dome. Rowen caught a
glimpse of a neatly made bed and the delicious smell of
food from the doorway between.

"Boys' rooms are back there. They've got this bug
about bein' neat. That's why I won't let 'em in here
much—they'd start cleaning so I'd never find a thing.
Kippy, let's have that chow!" In a moment Kip came in
with two steaming plates, with forks neatly wrapped in a
moist linen napkin. Rav studied his with a confused expression until Rowen showed him how to unwrap the
utensil and use it to move the red beans from plate to
mouth.

"Have a seat anywhere that's flat, fellas." She
shoved out a clear space on her long workbench with her
forearm. "I'll work while you eat, if you don't mind."
Kip returned with another pan of perfectly browned
biscuits. Rowen tasted the beans, then surrendered to
his hunger with the thought that he had not appreciated
food this much in years. Meanwhile Rav drank an entire
jug of water, with Kip standing by obviously impressed.

"Okay, Kippy, you go do what you want. You're off
tonight. These two got their hands full." Kip smiled,
whispered something as he kissed her cheek, then went
out.

"He's got a young lady-friend. Thinks I don't know.
But we'd be in a bad way if we didn't believe we're
smarter than our parents. Ain't that right, froggy?"

"I'm no more frog than you are cow, lady," Rav
said, not looking up from his food.

"You're a smart one!" Yannika had taken the deactivated Janoo from Kip's sack and was spinning open its
case lugs with a whirring power driver. "You sure you

caught him out of the sea?''

"From what he's said, his people have a thriving culture.''

"Thriving!'' She removed the lower half of Janoo's shell and pulled her work light over for a better look at the damaged works. "Fish in the water, sheep on land, neither one of 'em needs a brain. Breeder's all they are.''

"Better than being slaves to the sky gods, growing food to feed the hunters who steal from my world.'' Rav said.

Yannika's eyes narrowed as she pointed her driver at Rav. "Hoo, boy, that's fast talk. We kicked the Citizens out ten years ago. We're free, and we aim to stay that way.''

"And I've come up here to help free my . . .'' He hesitated. "My people.''

"Which is why you and I *might* be able to get along, if you watch your mouth. I've raised seven boys, all of 'em bigger than you. So mind you show old Yannika some respect.'' She probed Janoo's panels with forceps, squeezed on an eyepiece, and traced a connection. "There!'' she grunted. "Just like I thought. The memory-data interface is shot.'' She got a rolling ladder, pushed it through the junk on the floor to the shelves, then mounted it to retrieve a bin full of parts, bringing it back to the bench.

She rummaged through the bin. "I suppose you noticed I had a change of heart about you two out there. Part of it was your story. Citizens from Meems don't have that kind of imagination. Even if they did, they sure as hell wouldn't have called after one of these.'' Yannika held up a dark saucer whose rim was formed of folded-in claws. With minor variations, it was a replica of Rowen's Xein. "Upstairs—used to be here, too— these things used to help the Citizens' Police keep everyone in line. Do everything from cuttin' through doors to shooting a bolt through some poor bastard's heart. Things used to buzz around here like bees. Getting rid of 'em took some doing, until I tuned the field around my fence to overload their processors. Yours made it through okay, which meant it was set up different than the others. The antique battery was all the proof I needed."

Opening the second carapace, Yannika found a compatible unit and plugged it into Janoo's boards. Then she replaced the damaged top with a shell that was dented but still intact. "Won't be able to help you with the eye. But it should be able to compensate. Let's give it some juice."

As soon as she inserted the battery, Janoo retracted its claws and swiveled its one good eye around the shop, halting when its sensor recognized Rowen. One quick burst and it lifted off and swung joyfully around the shop once before settling excitedly onto Rowen's lap.

"You're back! Oh, how do you feel? Better? Well, that nice lady's the one that fixed you. Now, tell me where you were so long—"

Rowen halted. The Xein's excitement had turned to confusion. Somehow it was not able to transmit the data properly.

"Something else must be burned out in there."

"What are you talking about?"

"His temporary files won't purge."

" 'Course they won't. Those were wiped clean when the bolt hit him. You're lucky the rest of his programming's intact." She poured herself a cup of hot tea from a pot set on a hotplate near the doorway. "Anyhow, I can tell you more about this terrace than that thing could. I've lived here ninety-seven years. My family's been farming as long as Gaelen's been First Speaker."

The name of his old rival brought back the tragedy of Conteirre to him—and his plans to overthrow the Motherhood, if he possibly could.

"There's been one man of that name? Or a series of Speakers who have used it like a title?"

Yanikka slurped tea loudly. "That I can't tell you. All his pictures and images look the same, even when I run antique tapes. Who knows what goes on up there? I've got enough to worry about keeping the Free Zone in one piece."

"When you . . . farmed for the Citizenry . . . did they control your behavior mentally to make sure you did what was necessary?"

"You mean with the Mind? Naw, it'd take too much for the Mother to control everyone in the Slot direct. Especially when it takes most of her strength to hold off the powers beyond this world. No, they've got the police to keep everyone in line."

"So how do people survive?"

"As best they can, that's how! There's plenty of work to do, machinery to keep runnin', goods to move. A couple million fishies in cells to keep alive. Oh, they're busy all right, and as long as they do their work, they're left alone."

Rowen thought a moment. "Yannika, let me ask you something. Do you think they'd support a revolution?"

"Revolution!"

"Overthrowing the Mother. Killing the Mind without killing the people who are part of it."

"It's been tried. Look at the boy there if you want to see how successful it's been. Look at me!" She finished her tea and slammed the cup scornfully onto her bench.

"It wasn't the right time. Sinom—the Mother—was too strong."

"That ain't changed. She takes more and more of Rav's kind upstairs every year."

"But she's faltering. The fact that you've been able to maintain your Free Zone—"

"Is because I know my stuff. We've got a field that knocks down their floaters, and once they're down, they're dead Citizens. They don't dare show their faces around here."

"I'm trying to tell you the Mind's diseased. We've a good chance of defeating it if we strike now."

Yannika shook her head. "Strike now, eh? Why should we? We've got it good enough as it is."

"Do you? What kind of security do you have for the

future? Maybe the Mother hasn't got around to noticing your little rebellion yet. What happens when she does? That field of yours won't stand up to a full-scale military assault. You'll end up in worse shape than before you broke away. Assuming that the life-support systems haven't broken down for good."

"Talk's cheap, Speaker. What do you propose?"

"Help me organize a force. You've weapons and transport here, and manpower. I believe an assault on Meems is possible. A direct strike at the Mother herself. Once she's eliminated, the Mind breaks down again to its individual parts, and we can get on with the business of repairing our world."

Yannika chuckled, raising a hand to cut him off. "Save your eloquence, egghead. You might convince *me*, but the Zone's a democracy. If you're willing to stand before a general meetin' and tell my people what you've been tellin' me, I'm willing to go along with whatever they decide. Just keep in mind that if it's thumbs down, that's it. And they still might want to throw you over the edge—they're a feisty bunch. You take your chances, golden-tongue.

"What do you say, Rav?"

"All I care about is getting to Meems."

Rowen rose dramatically to his feet. For the first time since his resurrection, he felt like the First Speaker of the Citizenry.

"Call your meeting, Yannika," he said.

CHAPTER 21

The Electors of the Midlands Free Zone gathered in a building that in Citizenry times had been a freight distribution station. Now it housed a food processing kitchen and a small arsenal of floaters—some with mounted cannon—and stores of small arms, communications equipment, power units, and ammunition. Rowen stood with Yannika as the farmers came in out of the evening damp. They shook out steaming cloaks, stomped their boots, lighted pipes, and accepted cups of hot tea from a battered urn Ruthel had brought in. As the level of noise inside the building increased, Rowen found his nervousness also rising.

Preposterous, that he should fear speaking before such a small meeting. But he was afraid. Here he no longer had the luxury of being able to take his audience for granted. Here were people who did not believe in his influence or power, people who carried no reverence for his office or his reputation, people who cared nothing for the Conteirre he had known. How could he possibly reach them? What appeal could he construct that would convince them to go along with his vague plans to overthrow Sinom's rule? They would be risking everything

—on the word of a stranger who appeared to have nothing to lose himself.

Just then he caught an instant of sense from Janoo's jumbled transmissions. Tyron's name. The Xein still wasn't capable of answering Rowen's query, but the name suddenly gave the Speaker an idea. He lifted Janoo from his shoulder and handed it to Rav.

"Hold him, please. I don't want any of Yannika's friends shooting at him again."

"They should shoot at you instead?"

"That's a chance I take, stepping in front of any crowd." He saw Yannika waving her arms to silence the meeting.

"Pipe down!" She waited until they did. Then, "This won't take long. I've called you here tonight because we need an extraordinary vote of all the Electors of the Free Zone. The two strangers we caught this morning—Rowen and the fish boy there—have something to say. When they're done I'll put their proposal out for your formal vote. Dots and circles, as usual. Paper 'n' pens are over by the eats with the ballot box. Any questions?"

"Yeah," somebody yelled. "Where's the brandy?"

"You, Lapic, are the last boy I'd ever tell! Now shut up and let the man speak. And you like what he's sayin', save your energy for markin' ballots. Okay, I introduce Rowen, who claims to have been First Speaker before Gaelen."

Rowen stepped forward to the deck railing to laughter and murmured disbelief. Out of habit, he gazed for a few moments at the crowd. There were perhaps two hundred people, dressed not in the neat uniforms of the various classes of Citizens but in a motley of homespun and cast-off ornamented with leather belts, printed scarves, dirty overalls, bulky knit sweaters. The faces were worn. Some were downright hostile, some amused, some merely bored.

"Citizens of Conteirre," Rowen began, in a voice that would have rung from the dome of the Diet Hall.

Too much. He lowered his voice and began an account of the activities of the Committee of Two Hundred. Warming to his task, he shifted to the false promises of Sinom. "She claims there exist other Minds that populate the metaphysical universe. Her hope was to join with these minds, to gain supreme power. Supreme power for her, at the expense of her fellow Citizens.

"That's why we kicked her out!" A voice from the front. "Tell us something new!"

"I believe now that we have the opportunity to cut this cancer from our midst. To cleanse ourselves and rebuild the world anew. It will not be the first time our Citizenry has risen from the ashes of fiery destruction, and it will not be the last. The power of the Mother and her Mind will be, can be, *must* be broken. It is the duty we have to those who lived and sacrificed before us."

"The hell with duty!" Emphatic agreement from the crowd. "We've done our part already."

"Which means you have more strength than the others. Which gives you the responsibility—" I'm losing them.

"The only responsibility we've got is to sit tight and enjoy ourselves. We're living good; nobody's bothering us. So why should we throw it away to run off after somebody who could be a crazy man for all we know."

"Because it's *time*. The Mind's never been weaker than at this moment. She'll fall if only we have strength enough to push her over the brink."

A woman stood up. "If she's so weak, dying like you say, then why should we do anything? Sooner or later she'll be gone, and we won't have to risk a thing."

"That's right!" The noise came up, so loud that Yannika had to step in front of Rowen and give out an ear-splitting whistle before they would pay attention again. Shaking her head, she gave way to Rowen for what he knew would be the last time. But something the woman had said gave him a clue. Ignoring the past, these Midlanders naturally feared the future. He waited now until all were staring at him, challenging him to continue.

"You're farmers here. You can judge when the rains will come up from the sea. Or position your crops to best catch what light filters through that sky of ice. To you the world works because it has to, because it's a system, a self-perpetuating whole. But this canyon is an artificial refuge. It was designed to function in a certain way, and it's sustained by machinery that automatically maintains the balance necessary for human life to survive inside it. In my day that balance was tended by computers. Now the Mind controls the wind and the warmth and the light. And see what sort of job it does! Across from you—we traveled it—is a desert where farmland even more productive than yours once stretched along half a dozen whole terraces. Above you a ceiling of ice that every day seizes more and more of the moisture you need to live inside this canyon. This world is running, but badly. And if the Mother dies, this world dies with her."

That's it. "No more water surging through the penstocks to drive turbines for you; no more energy net across the mouth of the canyon to keep the air inside. This basin will dry up while the winds of this planet fill it with sand. That's what your gift to your children and grandchildren will be. Sand, your legacy for failing to strike when striking was possible." The faces looked stunned now, as though Rowen had pointed out something they had never thought of before. They were open, though maybe not for long, so he drove home his will with all the strength and skill at his command.

"Look around you. I see weapons here. Why did you store them if you never believed they would be used? And if they are to be used, is it not better to strike with them, strike before you yourselves are struck and pushed back into slavery? With these tools I can help you to free this world. Banish this evil thing that has had it in her loathsome grip for far too long. Let the Older Ones take what they will. This world belongs to us!"

At the last word, he turned away sharply and took refuge behind the steam kettle.

Yannika took the rail. "All right!" she yelled, breaking the spell Rowen had woven. "We vote for military assistance for the Speaker. Yes or no!"

"How do you vote, Yannika?"

"For me to know and you to find out. Make up your own minds, people. That's what we broke away for in the first place."

She came back to the platforms where Rowen and Rav waited. "Outside while they're voting, boys. Come on, I'll keep you company." They went through a side door into the cool evening. Across the canyon the last of the phosphor glow from the low deserts flickered across the dunes. Farther up, the terraces hung stark and heavy with the weight of snow. Only the ice vault continued to shine, and there was a faint roar from the falls at Heaven's Gate. Yannika lighted her pipe and blew out a steamy plume of fragrant smoke.

"Gotta hand it to you, Speaker, you know your stuff."

"Do you think they'll agree?"

"Can't say what they'll do. Takes a certain something to bring these folks together. They made the decision to fight once because they were up against a wall. It's not like that now."

"But it is."

"So *you* say. You're askin' an awful lot. Maybe more than they're prepared to give. But at least you've won safe passage for yourself and the frog. And I'll outfit you if you care to go on."

Kip looked out the doorway. "Vote's counted, Ma."

"Don't stand there with your tongue hangin' out! How'd it finish?"

"Yes one fifty-seven, no twenty-three."

"Damn!" Yannika slapped her thigh. "Looks like you've got yerself an army, Speaker!"

Rowen turned to hug Rav, but the boy had already stalked angrily away.

CHAPTER 22

Dink Morgan's limousine lay hidden in a stand of reedy red-trunked trees up the terrace from the city of Meems. The ground trembled here because of the tremendous penstocks set into the canyon wall half a mile farther up-slope. Jesse could hear hangers rattling in Morgan's closets. He'd been hiding here almost five hours now, waiting for something to happen. More ships, word from Katya, anything that would require action; he was good at that. At thinking, waiting, worrying—worrying most definitely—he was not so good.

Finally Jes decided he'd waited long enough. He opened the hatches and went outside.

Meems was much warmer than the other terrace had been, but there were still bunches of dagger-sharp icicles hanging from the girders of the covering terrace. Out past the city the cloud tops were sheared flat by the loop of circulating air dropping over toward the dry side of the canyon. There was the sound of water trickling from a nearby spring, and in the background, the deep, throaty whisper of tons of wind sweeping down-terrace from the canyon wall. Jesse kicked at the turf. A few hundred yards away was the grassy mound and the dark trench cutting into it. Between that mound and the

grove of red trees lay a jagged crevasse protecting the
mound the way a moat protects a castle.

The soft voice he had first heard on Morgan—the
voice that had promised to make him like Katya—lived
inside that mound. The voice had been silent a long
time. But it watched him now, Jes knew. He walked
toward the fracture and stopped at the edge. Not too
fast, he told himself. Don't be too anxious. That was or-
dinarily a good rule. Somehow, though, it sounded
hollow in this place.

A warm updraft from deep inside the fissue ruffled
his hair. There was an old footbridge a few yards away.
He went over to inspect the rotting planks and frayed
support ropes, and decided it would never hold his
weight. And the fault was too wide to jump. Morgan's
ship still had a little charge left; Jes decided to use it and
fly closer to the mound. When he turned, he heard the
voice inside his head. Gentle, but very, very loud.

Use the bridge, the voice said.

Jes turned back. The wind came up again, but there
was no sign of life from the mound. This was crazy!
Was he supposed to kill himself because he heard words
inside his head?

*Use the bridge! I could have killed you on Morgan's
planet if that is what I wanted. I could kill you where
you stand.*

"It'll never hold me!" Jes yelled toward the mound.

If you have courage, it will hold.

Jesse considered the situation. He'd left Kat behind
already. He didn't really fear for her safety—she had
too much going for her to be in real trouble, even in a
snowstorm. But he knew that after what he'd done,
things would never be the same with them. He'd blown
it. Was he going to blow this chance now too?

He went to the bridge, took a deep breath, grabbed
the anchor posts, and jumped. The plank he landed on
in the middle of the span snapped as he sprang again.
He could feel the rope coming apart with his hands as
the whole structure swung and twisted and then fell
away, leaving him in midair for a moment that was too

long. Then he hit turf on the other side and clawed his
way to safety.

Excellent. Now come into my house.

He got up, wiping his palms on his pants. His heart
hadn't got the message yet that he was out of danger.
There was no way back across the fissure now that the
bridge was gone. No choice for him, really, but to go
forward. So he approached the mound. Now he could
see the mouth of the trench, which was almost covered
by pale, lobe-leafed shrubs. Some of them had white
flowers whose pistils and stamens looked like the features of human faces, smiles dusky with violet pollen.

The walls were of sandstone slabs that had been
carefully cut and fitted together without mortar. Their
surfaces were carved into a weathered procession of
men and women in lizard masks. Closer to the doorway
of the rock hut that lay beneath the mound the figures
joined hands while tilting their masks toward a polished
band dotted with starburst pits. On the next slab the
figures were gathered in a circle; it almost seemed as
though the eyes behind the masks were looking at him.
He thought he heard sounds—strange, pleading chants,
hisses, cries for help, warnings that this was a place
from where no one ever returned—

"Welcome, Jesse Wallace!"

The voice, but no longer inside his head. He looked
away from the carvings and saw a woman—he thought
it was a woman—shrouded all in white. She sat in a
wheeled chair between the two deep black stones that
supported the doorway to her house. These stones had
no carving on them; they needed no carving, for by their
mass and caliginous color they radiated a stillness more
terrifying than the petroglyphs.

"Hello," Jes said.

"Please enter my house."

"All right."

"Mind not to touch these stones as you do." There
were small hesitations in her speech, as though it took
considerable effort for her to speak to him formally, in
words. Somehow the idea flattered him. "They are . . .

of a substance harmful to your kind.''

The chair motors whirred as she backed into the twilight inside the house. Jes followed her, and as his eyes adjusted, he saw that the ceiling was a dome formed of stacks of stone slabs finished with a capstone. There was a bed, and a chair, and a night table crowded with bottles and cups with spoons in them and paper tissues. It was like the bedroom any older person might have, except, perhaps, for the unit over the bed, where a cable was fitted that ran to the rear of the woman's wheelchair.

"You may . . . sit down," she said. Her body tensed—almost twitched—whenever the words faltered.

"I'll stand, if you don't mind."

Her veil was held with a tarnished starburst clasp, so that only one of her eyes showed. The dullness left that eye with his answer. Now the eye appeared amused.

"Everything on your terms . . . boy?"

"As much as I can get," Jes said. Ludicrous in view of his present surroundings. Feeling a little foolish, he sat down.

"As much as you can get," the woman in white repeated. "And what is it, precisely, that you have . . . come here to 'get', eh?"

"I think you know."

"Do I now?"

"You've been holding it out there ever since Morgan. Now stop playing games, lady. You wanted us down, and I got us down. You wanted me away from my sister, and I left her. Now I want my reward."

He watched the woman wheel over to the night table. Her brown, withered hand emerged from the white shroud, clasping a glass with a straw in it. There were sipping noises. After she set the glass down again she turned toward Jesse again.

"Reward? You think it a reward to be changed so that you are able to duplicate your sister's con . . . siderable talent? Think that will make your life complete?"

Jes shifted uncomfortably. "Something like that."

"You don't know what you're asking."

"I think I do. I've been with Kat long enough to know."

"Then why don't you realize how lucky you are not to bear the burden she bears? Think of it, Jesse Wallace. To have great power brings torment. How do . . . I use my power? Whom do I help, and, more importantly, whom do I ignore? The guilt, the terrible guilt of seeing injustice, poverty, degradation, and knowing you could do something, must do something, and when you do not, having that guilt pressing, gnawing . . . never ending. Failure! Pain beyond imagining! Oh, how lucky you are that you don't suffer as your sister and I do!"

"Save it! I've heard it all before. You're so special! Nobody else is good enough to do what you and Kat can do. All that means to me, lady, is simple greed. You want to keep what you've got for yourself, and to do that you use people. Arrange things. Make everyone fall right into line. Well, I'm sick of that! I want a life for me—Jes Wallace. I don't want to have to think about what Kat's going to say, or where Kat wants to go, or why Kat thinks I shouldn't be doing this or that. I want to be her equal. I just want my say for a change."

Her brown eye regarded him calmly, without blinking. She said sweetly, "It is no disgrace to devote your life to the care of another."

"That's fine. But I've done my bit."

"Your sister is surely worth a life. Especially a useless life. Your life."

Jes stood. "You're the type that doesn't keep promises, aren't you?"

"On the con . . . trary. I always keep my promises. I promised you life, and you'll have it, life that will take you beyond any of your puny conceptions of conjuror's tricks and confidence schemes. You'll have life, all right. As part of my Mind. And when your sister realizes that she must come here, to me, and help me complete our escape, we shall all of us go on to great things. As part of the Mind, you'll be far greater than if I gave you what you want right now."

"Sorry to disappoint you, lady, but I'm leaving."

"Stop!" He stopped. The grip of her will was far stronger than anything Katya had ever used on him. But it was much more desperate, and quickly withdrawn. He was looking at the stones that formed her doorway when she began speaking again.

"Those who enter the Mind do so . . . willingly. Coercion destroys much of what makes an individual mind useful to the whole. Coercion is also quite . . . painful. Now come here."

He felt the grip of her will tightening again. Beyond the animal fear it produced came clear thoughts, a moment of sanity. I left her alone for nothing! If I surrender now, she'll have to come, have to do anything the old woman says. And she will, just to save me.

Jes made his decision. He opened his mind and called Katty, warning her to stay away. Then he lunged for the stones. Their Cold burned his hands; he could sense the void that gripped the Mind here, and had seized the Mind of the lizard cult aeons before. They sensed him, gathering around, holding him, pulling him under. They would destroy him, not because they wanted to, but because his contact with their home would keep them from the abyss. By surrounding him, he realized, they kept Sinom from taking him herself.

You can't touch me! His triumphant cry as the Lost Mind pulled him away.

In the hut, Sinom breathed a curse, feeling the deaths of a thousand encelled minds with the effort of what she now had to do. She rolled forward to where the young fool screamed, gripped his arm, and, using the power of her motorized chair, pulled him off the stones and back into her realm.

"Useless though you are," she said, "I need what's left of you. I need whatever I can take."

She removed the veil. Then, with the calm born of ages, she took the head of the wild-eyed young man in her hands and forced him to gaze upon her face.

Book Six

THE COLD

CHAPTER 23

The weather had cleared while Tyron and Katya waited for the Xein to return. In the late afternoon the ice dome was a milky jade color, spidered through with branching fracture lines. Occasionally the ice growled and cracked, and when that happened, the whole terrace shook. Katya watched the spume falling from the vent Jes had dropped their ship through and thought, What if that arch gave way? What would happen to the people who were left?

And then she heard her brother's warning and gasped.

"What's the matter, girl?"

Her voice trembled. "She's got him."

Tyron scowled, got to his feet. "Don't try going after him. She'd swallow you, too."

"I know. I know. It's just he was so frightened! Like a little boy."

The way he put his arm around her was as close to being shy as Tyron ever got. "He was doomed the moment he brought you here. You knew it. You must have told him too."

"That doesn't make it any better, Tyron. He's my brother. I . . . I just can't believe he's really gone."

"I know, child. And I'm very sorry for you. Sorrier perhaps than for the rest of this." He lifted his hands toward the heights. "At least we knew what Sinom was before we accepted her plans. But you must not despair, Katya. Your brother's cries—was there anything coherent in them?"

"Not words. Visuals. When we're in a hurry we use visuals—images. They're quicker than words." She closed her eyes and forced her memory to reconstruct Jes's last desperate burst. He'd been inside a dark, dome-shaped house. Stones on either side of the doorway, black stones. Touched them, waves of voices lost to the Cold—and, for an instant, the breaking of Sinom's power over his will.

Katya looked back at Tyron. "He was trying to tell me about the stones, Tyron! Somehow, when he touched them, this Mind couldn't have him. But it only lasted a moment. She pulled him away." Tears stung her eyes. "He wanted to keep her from taking him in! So I wouldn't have to fight. So I could leave."

"Yes! Yes, that's it!" Tyron spat into the ground. "That brother of yours may have redeemed himself after all."

"What are you talking about, Tyron?"

"Do you want him back?"

"You know I do."

"And are you strong enough to fight for him? To go where the old woman lives and take him from her?"

"I want to try."

"Then we'll travel to Meems now. Take some more of these." He started picking figs, filling his pockets and tossing extras to her.

"But I thought you wanted to wait for the crab—for your friend, Rowen."

"He'll find us soon enough. Having our breakfast in Sinom's house, by stars! Let's go!"

An hour later they'd reached the very top of the terrace, where the ruins of a once bustling freight terminus

lay hidden in tangled vines and piles of scree fallen from
the rock walls. Tyron lead Katya to a bank of freight
elevators. Most of the doors were gone, and wind
howled menacingly up through the empty shafts. Near
the end of the complex, however, they located doors
that looked more or less in decent repair. Tyron opened
a panel cover and jiggled a few connections; after a
spark or two raised the sharp smell of ozone, the doors
opened with a gut-wrenching squeal of unlubricated
bearings and slides.

"Are you sure it's safe?" Katya asked dubiously.

"Of course it's safe! The platform's here—that
means the air column in the tube's still sound." He
stepped inside to show her, and the platform rocked
slightly. "Step aboard! *She's* not about to let you take a
fall now."

Reluctantly Katya complied, grabbing a padded
bumper that protected the shaft's glass wall. Tyron
threw some switches; moments later the door snapped
shut with a loud hiss and the lift slowly began to rise.

"Sit down, have something to eat. The trip will take a
while.

Katya sat. She watched Tyron eating some figs and
wondered what Dink Morgan would have thought of
the old man wiping his chin with the sleeve of that ex-
pensive fur coat.

Finally she said, "All right, Tyron. Now suppose you
tell me why you changed your mind so fast."

"Your brother's last message." He spit out blue rind.
"I should have seen it before. It's the stones."

"What about the stones?"

He swallowed. "You know about how those men
from the Committee tried to take me at my house?"

Katya nodded.

"I put my hands on the stones and felt the Cold for
the first time. And I felt the presence of the people who
built this world and who carved the sandstone blocks I
was investigating. They were desperate to escape, tried
to use me to pull themselves out of the void."

"I remember," she said softly, still embarrassed by how she had extracted that information from Tyron's mind.

"Sinom's men put me into a cell exactly like the cells on the Meems terrace. And I survived there until you found me. But I was not part of the Mind!"

"But you were linked. I had to break the connection when I pulled you from the cell."

"Linked, yes, but to the aborigines! I was part of *their* trapped consciousness. Their Mind made it impossible for Sinom to have me. Perhaps that's the reason my cell didn't fail when the others around it did. That's what your brother was trying to tell you. The aborigines will protect you."

"But you went mad—"

"Yes, and your brother would have suffered the same fate. Their power and agony was too much—like trying to capture that fall of water up there in a drinking cup. Too much for Jesse, or for me, but not for you. You have the capacity and the power to control that Mind. That's why Sinom wants you. *She* can't do it alone, but if she can get you to help her add the power of the aboriginal consciousness to the one she directs . . ."

"She'll be able to pull free."

"Exactly. So we must ask ourselves, girl, whether the Cold was created for a purpose. To keep the rest of the universe safe from beings of tremendous power and no conscience."

"What if it's only an accident?"

"Such a useful metaphysical condition seems unlikely to be an accident. But for the sake of argument, assume it is. Will you help Sinom to escape for the sake of your brother? What does your instinct tell you?"

She didn't hesitate. "No."

"Then the alternative is to destroy her. Separate her from the Mind. Let the Cold take her. Let the universe protect itself."

"But how could I do that? I've felt her power. You've said yourself she'd swallow me up."

"Your brother gave you the answer to that question.

The stones. *You* control the aboriginal consciousness, use its power to make you Sinom's equal. That way you may be able to rescue your brother—and free this world as well.''

Katya shook her head. If only she had time to think.

Then the lift stopped. Tyron scowled. "Did you do that?"

"No. Tyron, look! The door's opening."

"We can't be at Meems yet." He got up and jabbed at the switches, but the lift stayed where it was. Outside the door was darkness and thin, acrid air that burned inside Katya's nose. The old man swore.

"Tube's probably blocked. We'll have to use another one. Come along."

Katya followed him outside. Twisted evergreens were silhouetted against the pale green of the ice vault. A twig snapped. Then lights blazed in their faces. Katya heard excited shouts in the sibilant Conteirre language, which she could understand through Tyron. The meaning would have been clear in any case.

"Move and you die, Archaeologist!"

"Gaelen? Is it really you?"

"Yes, old man, it's me." His golden hair seemed to blaze with the radiance of a dozen suns.

Tyron spat in his face. Slowly, white with anger, the First Speaker wiped his cheek with the back of his hand. Then he lashed out with a blow that sent Tyron to his knees.

"Welcome back to the Citizenry, Tyron! Take them!"

CHAPTER 24

The lights at Yannika's dome burned deep into the night as she and her sons, along with a half-dozen squad leaders from the Free Zone defense forces, planned their assault on the Mother's city—Meems. Kip and Ruthel had—with a certain amount of satisfaction—cleared the big workbench of junk. Now it was covered instead with maps of the Meems terrace taken from engineering archives through Yannika's rigged link to the canyon's surviving computer banks.

Their plan had emerged after several hours of intense and sometimes angry discussion between Yannika and Rowen. Finally a two-stage assault had been agreed upon. First, the creation of a diversion by the capture of Hydraulic Control Unit Six, which housed the only working control and monitoring equipment for the on-surface pumping and mirror systems. Then, once the diversion had been created, a single strike in force at the Mother's house at the archaeological dig.

Yannika had already decided what the diversion would be. "I've been at that unit. It was during engineering school. They showed us that the main drives for the Dragonsback were still operational. Don't use them

now because of the ice cap, but they'll move. I'll make
'em move! And when that beam of sunlight bounces
down onto the cap, there's gonna be one hell of a
flood!'' Yannika winked at Rav. "Just what you like,
eh, froggy?''

Rav, who had been watching in sullen silence as the
plans took shape, suddenly bristled. "I told you not to
call me that!''

"Simmer down, sea boy! I don't mean anything by
it.''

But Rav had already stalked out of the dome.
Seething, he followed the glowing force field for a few
yards, then sat down to think things through. Ever since
Rowen had won the farmers over with his speech it had
become very clear that the sky god's mind was on other
things besides his promise to help Rav find Luci. Surely
what Rav wanted was of less importance in the
Speaker's view than what the Midlanders were prepar-
ing to sacrifice. Rav was just part of the background
now, someone to be taken care of when important matters were settled.

Rav looked up and saw that the morning light was
just beginning to divide the sky. Somewhere above the
dark presence of the next terrace was Meems—and
Luci. Rav had no idea how long it might take him to
reach the city on foot. But at the rate Rowen and the old
woman were finishing their plans he might well beat
them there if he left now. He only needed a way through
the fence and—

"Rav?'' Rowen came toward him with long,
deliberate steps. Everything about the man's exagger-
ated! "Is anything wrong?''

"What could be wrong now?''

"I thought perhaps you might be feeling the effects of
dehydration. Yannika's got a tub, if you'd like to soak
for a time.''

"For how long?'' Rav said bitterly. "Two days? A
week? We'll still be here a week from now, so what's the
hurry?''

"Rav—" A sigh.

"Don't waste your golden words on me, sky god—I know what they're worth. You're plotting conquest now, when you should be helping me find Luci."

"It's not that simple a matter."

"Isn't it? Everything else seems simple enough for you."

"Rav, I know the waiting is difficult. But you must realize that if the Mother does have Luci now, you and I couldn't get her back without help—the help these people are willing to give. We can't do it alone."

"And how would you know that? How could you know what it's like to have the Mother for an enemy, to have her take what you've lived your whole life for?"

"Because she took my wife!" Rowen grabbed Rav's shoulders and forced him to look at his face. "Yes, I know the feeling well. I left Mehga for little more than three hours, yet when I saw her again, it might have been three thousand years. Sinom had done something to her, *changed* her—*and there was nothing I could do to bring her back*. Nothing! I was First Speaker of the Citizenry, leader of a people who had journeyed a million million miles to make these ruins livable. They'd done it under my direction. But it made no difference. I was as helpless then as you are now."

"But you survived, didn't you?" Rav felt his anger slipping away against his will.

"*We* survived. And now *we* must do our best to take back what belongs to us. I need you, Rav. This is your world now, not mine. I'm a stranger here. Come back and I'll make certain we'll find Luci as soon as everything's in position in Meems. Come—please—I'll prove it to you."

As though Rowen's words had paralyzed his resolve, Rav allowed the First Speaker to lead him back inside the dome. Yannika grunted when she saw them.

"We've found the floor plans for Unit Six," she said. "Ruthel's running off copies right now."

"Good. Rav is to be in charge of the security team

outside the unit once we've taken it.''

"What? Now just a minute—''

"And if you'll excuse me a moment, Yannika, I need to consult Janoo verbally.''

The frowning Mechanic stepped aside as Rowen addressed the Xein, its one good eye popping up as Rowen switched it to its verbal mode. "Janoo, I want you to see if you can gain access to the records dealing with the occupants of the cells on the Meems terrace. We're looking for a recent arrival, processed sometime within the last two days. From Weiring—pardon me, W'ring—a young girl named Luci, fair-haired, a little larger than the norm.''

Janoo buzzed and began generating blips on the terminal screen. Looking red-faced, Yannika hitched up her overalls and declared, "We didn't agree to any fish-hunting up there. And I don't like bellyachers holding up the show.''

"I owe my life to this boy, Yannika. And we've agreed to search for his friend only after our primary mission is complete.'' He lowered his eyes at Rav. "Correct?''

"All right.''

Yannika scratched her head. "For a fast talker you've got a lot of patience. More than me—I'd let him go if he's so damn set on goin'. None of the responsibilities, none of the benefits—that's our motto here.''

Janoo suddenly beeped. Rav stared at the symbols on the screen, waiting for one of the others who knew how to interpret them for him.

"No record of her,'' Rowen said.

"What does that mean?''

"Could be dead, for one thing,'' Yannika said drily.

"Or that she hasn't yet been placed inside a cell. Which could very well improve our chances of recovering her—after we disable the Mind.''

"Brother, what a diplomat,'' the old Mechanic said. "Well, let's get the equipment together, folks. We'll leave tomorrow at dark?'' Her question was directed to Rowen, who looked at Rav.

"Tomorrow at dark. And fates willing, we'll have our world back at next light."

Yannika spent most of the morning outfitting seven of the reconditioned floaters with various pieces of weaponry left behind by the Citizens' Police in their hasty withdrawal from the Free Zone several years before. Most were capacitance-release beam cannons which drew on the floaters' batteries. A few shots would slow them down considerably, but it was the best Yannika could do on such short notice. Not wishing to leave her fleet completely powerless in the aftermath of a heavy exchange, Yannika equipped the lead and rear ships with bomb launchers driven by chemical charges.

"I've left the lightest one for the security team," Yannika explained as she surveyed her work. "Rav and my two boys'll have sidearms only. If we get in trouble they can peel off—this'll beat anything the Citizenry's running—and wait for another chance. Now we all better get some rest. We'll meet over at my place suppertime and go over the whole thing one more time."

Back at the dome, Ruthel filled the tub for Rav and left him alone to sleep in the warm, fresh water. His pores seemed to open to take in the moisture, and somehow the passage of water rather than air through his mouth and doubled lungs took away his anxiety. Closing his eyes he could almost imagine himself back home in W'ring, floating in the sea cave with Luci, but this time without the fear of the hunter ships to gnaw at his contentment. He had seen the ships, touched them, and survived. He had proven himself stronger than the sky gods had ever imagined. Rav's fingers closed around the ancient coin he wore like a medallion on the sea-grass thong around his neck. The face on that coin, he knew now, was that of Raeger, Rowen's own father, whose once powerful features had been worn beyond recognition by time and failure. No doubt there were other coins scattered beneath the sea floor with Rowen's image scoured the same way—smooth, glittering testimony to a world that had given up. Rav would not let himself be guided by such faded brilliance; his course was set with Luci as his star, and if the sky god chose to try to steer him another way, then the sky god would travel his way alone. Rowen had had his chance, and failed. Let Rav now have his own chance!

After a dreamless, timeless sleep, Kip came in to wake him for the final briefing. Rav stood up, blew water from his vents, then put on the quilted suit without first drying his body. He wanted to feel the touch of water against his skin to remind himself of his purpose, of the life with him he intended to return Luci to.

The others were already waiting for him in the workshop—five soldiers for each of the six escort floaters, plus Yannika and her boys and Rowen. Janoo sat on Rowen's shoulder, purring loudly as the Speaker examined a map and absently stroked the Xein's newly polished carapace. When he looked up and saw that Rav had arrived, he turned to address the rest of the group.

"First I'd like to thank you all for your enthusiasm and for your cooperation. Yannika tells me you've been drilling hard all day. I'm sure you're feeling a bit fagged if she's been barking orders at you." He paused to let the laughter die down. "She's made you aware of two things vital to the success of this operation. First, our total advantage of surprise. The Citizenry is not expecting us, Zoneers, and that increases our power a thousandfold. If we employ our speed and maneuverability as well, we'll be able to secure this installation without firing a shot."

"Now, Janoo will lead us up toward the Meems Terrace." He pointed to the chart. "There's an access conduit for structural inspection and repair large enough to accommodate us. Janoo's already ordered the computer to open the hatch up at Meems, and with any luck we'll emerge here—a few blocks away from the Diet of Citizens, and our destination, Hydraulic Control Unit Six. Once up, we'll assume our formation as quickly as we can: heavy cannons in the front and rear, two side escorts, and two on top. You'll be cupped over the unarmed floater with Rav and Ruthel. Hopefully we'll be able to fly low and under the cover of darkness to our objective. Remember that this is only the first stage of the operation. If you're hit, or run into something you can't handle, you're to break formation and take an evasive course to the rendezvous point here, up-terrace. Knocking out part of the Mind will do us absolutely no good unless we also deal with its director when we've finished at the Control Unit. So make it there if you can, and stand by for attack orders.

"All of you have your assignments and floor plans for the Control Unit. We'll enter through the large service entrance here, then the teams will spit up and each secure their assigned doorways. When we're finished you're to rejoin the force guarding the ships in the receiving area. When Yannika and I finish with the mirror controls we have our chance for some target practice at the archeological site near the terrace top. Do you have any questions?"

"Yeah. How do we know the Mother's there?"

"Yannika?"

"Because that's where the buzzer says she is, Clym. She's got support systems of her own, and that's where they run. I don't think she moves too well without 'em at her age." Yannika laughed, shaking her tangled hair, then held up her callused hands for silence. "There's something else I wanna say before we shove off. I wasn't too hot on this Citizen when we first caught him a couple days ago. But when I listened to him talk, well, he was sayin' things all of us knew but didn't want to admit to ourselves, know what I mean? This thing was meant to happen, and we were meant to do it. I believe that's why we were able to get free in the first place. Now's the time for us to start lookin' beyond, because if we accomplish what we're going up there to do, this Slot's gonna be a different place, and we're gonna have to help organize it. And I say there's nobody better to lead us than this Citizen here. So I move that we declare Rowen *our* First Speaker, 'cause damn his squinty little eyes, he sure as hell speaks for me!"

Rowen modestly lowered his eyes as the shout of acclamation shook the timbers of the dome. Yannika's
hearty backslapping he humbly accepted in lieu of a
crown.

"Now take yer positions, folks, and let's see what the
great Mother can do about it!" The strike force cheered
and went out to their waiting floaters. Rowen lingered a
moment, found Rav, and put his arm around the stripling's broad shoulders.

"Can you carry this rifle? Kip or Ruthel can show
you how to work it."

"I've already practiced, sky god."

Rowen smiled.

"Rav, I don't blame you for feeling used. I did use
you, and I can't apologize for it—that's what a leader
does. But there's something I want you to think about
while we're on our way to Luci."

"What's that?" Rav raised the rifle and adjusted its
strap.

"The people in the cells are your people. Sea people.
And they will need to be ruled by one of their own. I
would like to offer that job to you."

"I didn't know it was yours to offer."

"I'm not your enemy, Rav. Just think about it."

Kip stuck his head through the door. "Ma says we're
wasting fuel."

"We're coming. Rav? If you care for Luci, you've
got to care for her brothers and sisters, too."

Rav stepped around him. "We've made too many
promises already, sky god."

Watching him go, Rowen knew that he was right.

Rav sat in the middle seat of the unarmed floater as it
rose with the rest of the formation above the edge of
Terrace 18. Meems was the next one up, and even in the
darkness the boy could make out its structural differences from the others, the half-mile overhang whose
face resembled the faceted skin of a blackfish in the
faint glow from the ice vault. Inside each of the facets
lay a body, sustained by circulating fluid.

There were *sea people* resting inside that overhang, forming the Mind with the combined power of their individual brains. Together they had made something Rav could not completely understand, something which he had nevertheless promised to help destroy. And Luci might be among them. Janoo had said that she had not yet entered the system, but what if Janoo was wrong? And what would happen when the sky began to melt, sending storms of ice and hot water down past the terraces to the sea? He tried to put the thought from his mind, but his unease made it impossible. Should he kill Luci in order to rule the sea? Rav wished that Rowen was easier to distrust, easier to hate. There was something about him that inspired confidence in his judgment and his plans, even when Rav was unwilling to give it. Certainly the others in the strike force seemed happy to follow Rowen, and perhaps even to die for him, when less than two days ago they were demanding his execution with equal fervor. Then why couldn't Rav surrender in the same way? If only there were something about him to hate!

With Janoo leading the way, the convoy swung inland over a factory quarter. Everything was quiet. Yannika signaled for the pilots to close their formation. Then, moving as one, the floaters entered the service tunnel in the dark underbelly of Meems.

Along the way, cross tunnels were marked with red lights, a seemingly endless string of them meeting at a point that looked miles away. Gradually the point separated into two points, and then into a circle of red and amber at the egress to the Mother's city. Rav watched Kip nervously shift his rifle from shoulder to shoulder, and he himself felt the tension as the convoy slowed.

Then they rose out of the tunnel. Yannika's floater led the way north toward the Control Unit. They were leaving Meems, skirting the place, several miles from the service tube, where Yannika said the Mother lived. Rav had thought from the beginning that the convoy should destroy that place immediately. No one had

detected them, so why bother with a diversion? But
Rowen had convinced the Mechanic that Sinom's home
was hardly likely to be undefended, and that in any
case, the Mother would be able to sense the convoy
herself if it came too close, when she was otherwise un-
distracted. Rav watched the grid of streetlights from the
city recede. Luci was somewhere near. Yet the way
things stood, he had as much chance of finding her as he
had back in the sea, at W'ring.

The floaters skimmed the highway out of Meems
now, flashing past towers and blocky Citizenry-style
buildings, crossing empty side streets that seemed to run
the length of the terrace. Then, suddenly, came Yannika's signal to halt. In front of them was a metal half
dome that had been built over the cluster of six
penstocks. Streaked with corrosion and wet with condensation, these ran back to the canyon wall and then
shot upward into the frame of the next terrace. At the
opposite end of the building lay a complex of trans-
formers, heat exchangers, and power transponders.
Control Unit Six was perhaps the most important
building on the whole terrace.

It was also almost completely unguarded. The cowed
Citizens of Meems posed no threat to it, and the Meems
defense forces had long ago stopped worrying about attack from off-worlders or rebels from other terraces.
The drilling Yannika had put her squads through made
things even easier. They surprised three security guards,
disarmed them, and then locked them with the handful
of technicians who ran the plant in a storage room.
Meanwhile, Kip, Rav, and Ruthel, each armed with a
rifle and equipped with a hand-held radio, took up sen-
try positions along the front and sides of the building.

Dawn was just starting to illuminate the ice now.
Heaven, Rav had always called it, never dreaming that it
was nothing but frozen water. Water that would melt
and break up as soon as Yannika made the mirrors
work. Heaven melting . . . the Mother-house destroyed
with weapons . . . ice raining into the sea. What would
happen to his people? And what about Luci? If she were

already sleeping inside her cell, with the Mother in control of her mind and her soul, what would happen to her when the Mother was killed? The sky god claimed that Luci and the others would then be free, but Rav could not believe that. He knew the Mother was as vengeful as she was possessive. Hadn't she sent the black water to punish those who had opposed her rule? How then would she strike down those who dared to come to Heaven itself, seeking to kill her? Rav shivered, thinking about it. It was so easy not to believe in the Mother when one was living in the warm safety of the sea. Now he was not so sure of himself. He needed Luci. He didn't need the sky god and his promises of power, of a future where hunter ships no longer visited W'ring. Power was for the Mother, and he was a fool ever to have believed anything else!

Rav looked out over the glowing streets of Meems. From the maps, he thought he could find the place where Yannika said sea people were prepared for their lives inside the cells. Ruthel and Kip were both out of sight now; he was not scheduled to rendezvous with them for another eight minutes. Luci was out there, needing him, calling for him.

He made up his mind. He took the rifle from his shoulder and tossed it onto the street. Then he started back toward Meems, and Luci.

If love had any power left in the world, he would find her.

Rowen stood by as Yannika and one of the captured technicians worked at a pair of computer terminals in the valve room of Control Unit Six. Everyone had been issued with ear plugs, because of the howling turbines on the main deck below them, but Rowen had no need for words now. The look of intense satisfaction on Yannika's face told him everything he needed to know. Finally she slapped both hands on the panelboards, got up, and yelled her report when he pulled out one of his plugs.

"Okay, Speaker! We've got drives six, seven, ten,

fourteen, and nineteen turned on, all active. There's a couple others we're not sure of. Lost a lot of glass up there!''

"Will you be able to focus on this area?"

"That's what we got goin'. Sun's up in about ten minutes. We can crank 'em into position when you give the word.''

Rowen nodded. Then Kip ran in, breathless and worried, to yell something into his mother's ear.

"What's wrong?"

Yannika frowned, leaning toward Rowen. "Don't know if anything's wrong. But Kippy says the fish boy's left his post. No sign of him except his weapon, lyin' on the ground. Now ain't that one hell of a note! If the police catch him wanderin' around, they may finally wake up to the rest of us.''

"He can't have gone far. Janoo and I will go after him."

"While we sit here and sip our tea, I suppose!"

"We won't be gone long."

"How long?"

"I can't tell you that, Yannika—"

"Then I'll tell *you*. Twenty minutes. And if you ain't back by then, I'm cranking these mirrors and goin' on to stage two. With you or without you!''

Rowen saw arguing with her now would do no good. He agreed. Then he and the Xein left the building and set off after the boy from W'ring.

CHAPTER 25

Luci choked on the stagnant, perfumed water of Gaelen's pool, but she forced herself to breath. She had gone without water for too long, and she knew she must regain her strength if she wanted to leave this place before the sky god returned.

The wreckage of her grotesque makeup floated over her as she sucked in cleaner water from the bottom. Furiously, Luci rubbed her lips, still tingling from the mauling Gaelen had given them. When the last traces of the cream were gone, she scoured her face free of the powder. Then, cautiously, she surfaced.

The room was empty. Gaelen had left the door open, and Luci glimpsed uniformed sky gods passing along the hall. They took no notice of her. Trying to be quiet, she blew water from her vents. Then she considered her plight.

The sky gods, for all their size and physical beauty, were not the demigods her teachers had said they were. And Gaelen, their leader, reeked of insanity! How could the Mother have chosen such a man to be the physical agent of her divine power?

Unless, somehow, the Mother didn't know what the sky god had become. And how could that be possible,

when the Mother knew everything that happened in the
world?

Tortured by such conflicting thoughts, Luci rose
from the pool. Water ran from her soaked gown across
the alabaster floor. The slippers that Gaelen's atten-
dants had laced to her feet chafed, but she decided it
would be better to leave them on. Luci could not swim
any longer. She must walk, as the sky gods did, as her
ancestors had before they were sent into the sea to live.

She began a prayer to the Mother, but her doubts
were too strong, and she could not finish. Instead, she
thought of Rav. Darling, if you can hear me, I'm coming home. Please wait for me.

She could see Rav in her mind, and he gave her hope
as she left the chamber and followed the corridor out
the same way she'd been brought in. Sky gods passed
her, taking no notice. Luci followed some of them
through a cavernous entryway whose columns were
emblazoned with golden starbursts; then through glass
doors to the outside. There, shivering with the strange
cold air, she stood on the great stairway and looked to
the sky.

It was the same sky she had always known, but different as well. No longer just a stretch of pale green, it
was shot through with bumps and cracks like the floor
of the sea. And the Mother's Hand—hadn't Rav told
her once that it was only water—poured through a hole
in that sky, tossing rainbows to the winds. Water drifted
past the edge of the terrace. Falling—falling!—like rain,
down toward the sea.

Toward the sea. If this was the same sky, the same
Mother's Hand, the same line of green one could see in
good weather from W'ring, then it might be possible to
return home after all! The joy she thought had been
killed when the hunter ships had taken her burst into life
again, and slowly, fighting the heaviness of her body,
Luci walked past the seemingly endless facade of the sky
god's palace, toward the edge of the terrace.

It was a hard journey. The road stretched on and on,
and seemed to end in a piece of the sky rather than the

sea. Sky gods driving motorized carts passed her. Her chest burned, and once she stopped at a fountain to breathe water. Luci found it difficult to leave that fountain, but thinking of Rav drove her on until she finally reached a line of trees near a place where the road seemed to end. North of them she saw a place where the ground dropped away along a slanted edge that was divided into honeycomb cells. Taking shelter beneath a tree, where it was cooler and the ground still moist from the morning dew, she sank to her knees exhausted, and watched as crews of sky gods moved things from their carts onto cable scaffolds in front of the cells.

The things were the still bodies of sea people.

Luci gasped. One of the crews lowered its platform, then opened the front of a cell. Yellow fluid gushed out; then, as Luci's horror grew, one of the sky gods used a gaffing pole to yank out a gray, dead body and pull it onto the platform. After that they sprayed the inside of the compartment with a hose, lifted their living replacement, and quick as a cook slipping craws into a pot, shoved it inside and sealed the front again.

You will be taken to Heaven to be part of the Mother . . .

All her life she had believed that meant that the Mother would take her children into her home, to serve her and adore her. In return the Mother would give eternal life and freedom from the cares of the world. Luci had always imagined her to be a huge, gentle woman with the kindest of faces, who, with love and her divine power, transformed a single sea child into something like a god. And the transformation would be beautiful and mysterious, something holy. Not like this . . . meat storage . . . *cattle.* Rav's words came back to her with brutal force: *We're stockfish, Luci! Eaten up and then spit out again.*

"Citizen!" A harsh voice behind her. "This is a restricted area! State your business!"

Slowly, painfully, Luci faced a sky god who wore a white uniform—and a startled expression when he realized that she was not really a Citizen.

"I'll be damned! A fish that got away. You're not mindlinked yet, are you?"

Luci shook her head.

"Then you'd better come with me so you can be with the Mother."

"No!" She pulled away. The sky god shook his head.

"What's the matter with you? Don't they teach you froggies respect anymore? Get in that cart!"

"I said no!" Luci started running. Branches scratched her legs and arms, but she didn't feel them, only pushed forward toward the light. Then, suddenly, she emerged at the edge of the terrace.

Stones and dirt fell into the maw of the canyon, swallowed by swirling cloud tops. Luci watched them part, revealing a twisted serpent of cobalt blue lying on red sand. A serpent, far away, clouds between, the sky, the golden thread between the walls of the world that Rav said was a bridge from one place to another. And that serpent, so tiny, so blue, was home.

She stared at it. Rav must be there somewhere, along with her crèchemates and the Priestess Tahr, and the sea caves, and the ruined old city by the shore. Home. But how to get there? If only she could pray! But the Mother was evil, or dead and unaware of the evil that had swallowed the world. Could she fly home? Instinct—the instinct of a species that had once dwelt in trees, for whom falling was the greatest horror—rose faintly, warning her.

Then: "There she is! Don't move, fishie, we don't want you to hurt yourself. That's right. We're coming for you now."

To be put inside a cell, lying like a dead person, until you *were* dead and the sky gods hooked you out and threw you away. . . . One of them made a grab for her. Luci, without looking back, suddenly knew what she must do.

Closing her eyes, she pushed off the terrace with the last of her strength and felt herself fly. Toward W'ring. Toward home.

CHAPTER 26

The three ships escorting Gaelen's floater to Meems terrace peeled away when the formation reached the outskirts of the capital. Tyron watched them go; then he returned his gaze to the patch of green near the canyon wall. There Sinom lived inside the temple Tyron had been busy investigating when the course of his life was so abruptly and violently altered.

Only a few moments away now. Tyron squeezed Katya's hand. Was she strong enough to fight the old woman and win? Soon they would find out.

But then, suddenly, Gaelen changed direction, taking his floater over the city, away from Sinom's house. Now, for the first time, Tyron's anxiety showed.

"Where are you taking us?"

Gaelen forced a laugh. "What do you care, old man?" The floater lost altitude. They were gliding in toward the huge dome of the Diet Hall.

"Gaelen, listen to me! This girl can save our world. She's the only one who can take it back from Sinom without destroying what's left."

The Speaker leaned back. "Why should that matter to me? Pilot, put us down by my private entrance. I've got some uncompleted business to take care of." He smiled. "Whether you get to Sinom or not doesn't concern me. However, my wife has rebellious urges of her own. To satisfy them requires the presence of the girl. And no doubt it will amuse her to see you again, Tyron. Open the bubble."

The bubble did not rise. Angrily, Gaelen cuffed his pilot's head. The man did not so much as flinch. He remained upright, stiff, hands locked onto the floater's controls. Tyron glanced at Katya and saw that her eyes were closed. Gaelen, furious at the pilot's supposed disobedience, reacted too late to avoid Tyron's sharp chop to his neck. He slumped forward unconscious in his seat. The bubble opened. Stiff as a marionette, the pilot left the floater and walked away. Tyron wasted no time taking his seat and getting the craft into the air again. He headed west, back toward the circle of green. Closer to it they could see the fissure and the remains of the footbridge. It was strange for Tyron to recall Rowen's final visit here—and how hesitant the First Speaker had been to cross that bridge.

"Look! There's the ship." It rested on the border of the turf, looking pale and battered in the artificial light. Tyron cut power and brought the floater down on the other side of the crevasse.

"Think you're ready, girl?"

"I hope so. For Jes's sake."

"It will be difficult, Katya, but you must try not to think of your brother. Sinom will take your concern and use it against you. You must not be distracted. And you must be patient. Feel her out. Lull *her*. And, when the time is right, and only when you have to, then you must touch the stones. The touch will terrify you, but don't surrender to your fear. Overcome it. I do not think the cultists who built this place were evil by nature. If you are strong enough, they cannot harm you. And they will be grateful to do your bidding, if that can help them escape the Cold. Let them work through you—she won't be able to do anything to stop it."

Katya stepped out of the floater. "What about him?"

she asked, nodding at Gaelen.

"This traitor? It will be a pleasure to hit him again. As many times as it takes until you return."

"All right." She straightened, took a breath. The light spilling off the turf atop the mound was the color of bones. She walked forward and entered the trench.

On both sides the glyphs carved by the canyon's builders seemed to close in. Strange figures in lizard masks reached out to seize her. She felt dizzy. The arcade wavered before her eyes as though the whole thing were made of smoke. Then, suddenly, she visualized this terrace as it had been in the time of the aborigines: a natural ledge of caked sand marked by carefully tended ritual spaces, all of it guarded by the megalithic monuments. At the center, where the turf-covered hut presently lay, were the paired black stones. Katya could see these anchors, as they had been, and as they were now. She opened her mind, puzzling at the way they seemed to absorb everything.

They're machines! A link between the people who had built this place and the Cold. They knew what it was! They worshipped it, and, when at last they were able to soar with their minds above the mere physical world, they went to it, leaving the stones behind as their monument. And a way for them to contact the world, and those who came to it after they were gone.

Katya was at the door to Sinom's house. Slowly she brought up her hand—and then remembered Tyron's warning. Motors hummed in the dim light within the hut. Katya could see an unmade bed, and the smell of disinfectant and urine was strong, reminding her of a hospital she had worked in once on a planet called Oran.

"Hello, daughter."

She had never heard that voice, not like Jes had. But it was familiar all the same.

"Abbess?"

"Come in. I want to see you better."

Katya entered. Now she could see her, shrouded all in white, one eye showing. A shunt pulsing with blood ran from a control box above the bed into her arm.

"A long journey," Sinom said. "But you're here now, as I knew you would be."

"Where's my brother?"

"He's . . . safe. With me. For your sake I have taken him under my protection, where he can do him . . . self nor us any further . . . harm." She chuckled softly, almost sweetly. "So many years . . . I've called. But you would not answer me un . . . til you were ready. For the best. I have waited a long time to complete my work . . . to es . . . cape my enemy. It would not do to move too quickly. Before you could tru . . . ly help."

"We came here by accident."

"The concept of accident . . . is a fallacy, com . . . forting to minds more limited than ours, my dear. I called you many times. On Hexxan, on C-tau, Bar . . . kus. I watched over you when you lived at the found . . . ling's home on Danitz. And, of course, on Mor . . . gan's planet. You could have been happy there . . . with me. But we both had our responsibilities. You, your brother. I . . . this place . . . the millions . . . I care for." Suddenly the chair motors whirred and Sinom moved to her night table. She picked up a glass of green liquid that had a straw in it. She drank for what seemed like a long time; yet the level in the glass hardly fell. Katya thought, Can she be so feeble as this?

"I beg your pardon," Sinom said in a stronger voice. "It is difficult . . . to speak . . . this way. If we joined our minds . . . you would understand ev . . . erything . . . at once."

"Are you asking me to join you?"

Sinom's eye glittered. "Most humbly, Katya."

"I'm flattered, Lady, that you believe I can help. Something of your difficulty has come through to me. But before I agree to anything, I want Jesse back."

"Admirable loyalty. But useless. He has never done any . . . thing but drag you down . . . use you! I offer you a chance to fulfill your destiny. To become great along with me. To become what we were meant to become."

"And what is that?"

"Rulers of worlds. Creators. Yes, and where necessary, destroyers. Nothing is ever created without destruction. You can never go beyond what you are now without eliminating the pitiful hold your brother has on you. He's nothing, compared to you. I myself, if I had your power, would never have let myself be trapped . . . by the Cold. I would have . . . been able to pull away, before its hold on us became too strong." Sinom's head moved beneath the veil. "I . . . never dreamed any force could op . . . pose me once I linked with the necessary number of minds here. I had five . . . thousand of my first disciples . . . strong . . . wanting to do my . . . will. With them, I could am . . . plify my own powers . . . travel far, far beyond this poor world. I had a home up on the surface then, and I remember rising up, spreading my mind with growing confidence.

"And then it touched me! Just a brush at first, almost . . . curious about me. I thought, this must be the presence of an . . . other great Mind. Like a trusting child, I followed . . . traveling deeper, further than I had ever traveled, even in the days when I searched the heavens from the homeworld for a place of refuge for . . . the Citizenry. Far from home . . . far from the minds that gave me strength. . . . I felt it again! More . . . than a touch this time. Caught me, began pulling, and the more I resisted, the stronger the pull became!

"Imagine my terror, Katya. Imagine the desolation, the horror of suddenly realizing that everything was finished . . . that I would never es . . . cape . . . never use the Mind . . . I had built. There was nothing! Only Cold . . . empty . . . eternal.

"I've felt it too," Katya said.

"Yes. Through me. In . . . the end, my terror, and my smallness . . . only five thousand . . . helped me to escape. But the thing kept its . . . cold hand on me . . . waiting for the day . . . when I should . . . be . . . come powerful enough to be snatched away entirely.

"So I began to build . . . gain political control, so . . .

cial control of the Citizenry. Through Mehga, who had been the wife of First Speaker Rowen, and through Gaelen . . . more cells . . . more minds linked to mine. When it was . . . determined that normal pheno . . . types did not live long in sus . . . pension, we . . . produced variations . . . strain that lived in the sea on the can . . . yon floor. Bred in ig . . . norance . . . to serve me. The Mother!''

She laughed. The shunt into her arm pulsed, and Sinom herself stiffened, drawing her knees up. Katya stared, fearing the old woman had suffered a seizure. But then, gradually, Sinom relaxed again.

"The Mother. . . . A Mother who cannot break free without your help. You must help me! We're alike, you and I. Once I was a young girl, pretty, not caring for anything but the sight of my own face in a mirror. Then, one day . . . a stupid accident in my room . . . a fire— quite the opposite of my problem now—a fire . . . trapped, horribly burned. My parents were religionists . . . natural, not believing in tam . . . pering with fate. Refused . . . medical treatments. But no one, you see, could bear to look at me. I withdrew ever inward, frightened by the horror my face caused. And then, one day, when my despair became a thing that would devour me . . . because I had given it life . . . my mind came to life! I could enter the minds of others, put my own thoughts into their empty heads! I used the gift cruelly at first—as you did . . . to revenge yourself on those who hurt you. You . . . acted through your . . . brother. But the effect was the same. Only . . . later, did I realize, as you must realize now . . . that such power is never given out at random, for no purpose. It is our purpose, together, to defeat the Cold. To free ourselves. To come to life again . . . on high. To rule! That is our destiny."

Sinom whirred closer. "Come, Kat . . . ya. The time for evasion is past. Open your thoughts to me. Let me guide you . . . show you what must be . . . done."

Katya felt Sinom reaching for her. Frightened, she put down barriers. She knew they wouldn't last when the old woman finally began to bear down.

"First I want Jesse back. When he's safe, and off this planet—"

Gales of rage staggered her then. Not the rage of one mind alone, but the combined fury of every consciousness from every cell. Katya tried to fight back, but it was too much, too sudden. She needed power to protect herself. She needed the stones. Two steps away . . . hands out, ready for the contact with alien minds, with the mindless Cold that held those minds. . . .

"That's right, Katty! Go ahead. That's right up your alley, thinking of yourself first. To hell with me!"

He stood between her and the stones, looking hurt and angry, and frightened. Katya blinked.

"Jes?"

Yannika paced impatiently along the catwalk above the control Unit's turbine room. Soldiers of the strike force who had been holding their assigned positions for what seemed like hours now looked back at her nervously. Yannika couldn't blame them for that, but she tried to ignore their silent questioning. Finally, when she was about to roar with frustration above the howling machinery, her son Kippy rushed in. Together they went into the control booth, where things were quieter.

"Well?" she demanded.

"No sign of 'em, Ma. And the Speaker won't answer his radio, either."

Yannika cursed, then turned to the Citizenry technician who had helped her activate the mirror drives. "You! How much longer can we keep those hydraulics goin'?"

"Another five minutes. After that the pumps automatically cycle down to keep from overheating." He checked a panel and got a readout. "Looks like we've already lost number fourteen."

"Damn! Then we got no choice. Crank 'em!"

The technician flashed a grin. Starting the mirrors was a long-harbored fantasy of his. Yannika helped him throw the appropriate switches, then watched the pressure readouts rise and the temperature readouts steady.

Ten miles above them, on the sand-swept surface of Conteirre, gimbals that had not moved in nineteen hundred years groaned to life. Their designers had been very careful to seal the tremendous bearings and worm gears against the elements. After a moment's hesitation—a nod to inertia—the yokes that supported the mirror frames began to rise from the surface, spilling sand. The Dragonsback tilted to face the sun. And though mirrors were cracked and pitted, and some completely ruined, enough remained to reflect the light into a fierce, focused band. It caught the lip of the canyon opposite the mirrors. Then the band traveled down, sublimating frost and CO_2 ice in a smooth, steaming swath. A few minutes later the band of focused sunlight stopped, centered at the midpoint of the ice vault. Almost immediately the rivers and lakes cutting its surface began to heat up, then boil. Steam rose and refrosted the lip of the canyon.

The sky began to melt.

Back at the Control Unit, Yannika waited only long enough to make sure the mirrors were aimed where she wanted them aimed. Then she gave the order for the squads to reassemble at the rendezvous point.

Rowen or no Rowen, the Free Zone strike force was about to pay the Mother a little visit.

"Jes? Are you all right?" She wanted to hug him, but he kept his distance.

"You don't touch me!"

"Jes!"

"Jes," he sneered. "Always, Jes, why are you in trouble again, Jes, we couldn't possibly do something like that! Damn, I hate you! You've never cared about anything but yourself."

She didn't want to believe it was him, but the words hurt, and she had to reply.

"That's not true. I love you!"

"Yeah, you love me all right. Enough to let me rot here!"

"I came here to save you!" Her voice trembled.

"You were going to touch those stones, weren't you? Just like the old man told you to do! Did he tell you what that would do to me?"

You must forget about your brother. That's what Tyron had told her. Jes shook his head fiercely. "Yeah, he told you all right." Suddenly his expression changed. He looked frightened, as frightened as he'd looked that day on Hexxan when he'd brained their foster mother with the flatiron. "Please don't leave me with her, Katty. Please! I'm the only flesh and blood you've got left."

She put her hands to her ears. "Stop it! Stop it!"

"I'm not afraid to die, Kat, but not like this! Not rotting inside her! I know I've always screwed up, but I'll make it up to you if you just help me. We'll go anywhere you want . . . settle down. No more schemes, no more jealousy. Just take me out of the Mind. You can do it! I know you can, all I need's a little push." He held out his arms. "Help me, sis. Help me!"

Tears streamed down her face. Tyron's warning, Jes, what Sinom had told her—all were mixed together, and the only thing she could see clearly was him. She could not live without him. So she turned toward the lady in white and opened her mind.

Sinom's shriek of triumph faded just as the image of her brother disappeared and Katya's mind was torn from her helpless body.

CHAPTER 27

The Work Brigade Bridge leapt toward her, passed in a blur of cables and broken gold roadway, receded. Arms out, legs spread, Luci rolled to her back and watched it go. Now the sky was her sky again: the vault of Heaven, the hand-shaped spume of water, the banded colors that she knew now were farmlands and cities—and cells. Cells imprisoning the W'ring sea people.

Luci would return to the sea to warn the others. The cobalt-blue serpent was much broader now, speckled with whitecaps in crisscrossing arcs stirred by the winds. So beautiful. Did the hunters in their ships see this beauty as they descended to begin their harvesting? Luci doubted they did. Sky gods were too cowed to appreciate beauty. They could not love, could not even worship the Mother they feared so much. And, incapable of that, they could not work up enough hatred to overthrow her rule.

Sky gods had no heroes. No one strong enough to see the world through new eyes, the way Rav had. Did he still wait for her? Perhaps he was surfacing now, looking skyward as he blew out his water lungs. Luci felt happy, thinking of him free and strong that way. Sad, too, that they would never be able to live together as they'd planned. What children they would have made! But in a way, something new had been born of their love for each other. Rav had taught her to question the world, to follow her convictions, to do what was right. She would be inside a cell now if not for that.

She could see the ruined city on the W'ring shore quite clearly now, growing ever larger. Winds tore at her gown, at her hair. Luci embraced the winds, and thanked the Mother that she now knew what it was like to fly. Soon she would meet the water; whatever happened after that, she was certain of one thing: She would be home. And life, for those who found her, would never be the same again.

The rain began.

At first it was nothing but a gentle mist, blown inward and across the terrace by the ever present updraft. But very quickly the drops grew larger and the rain, which before had been brought by warm air masses rising from the ocean, fell more heavily than it did in the most severe storms. Soon it began pouring from the edge of the next terrace above Meems: a deluge of rain pummeling the city, turning streets into cold, churning rivers. And overhead, against the insane noise of the rain, the sky rumbled and cracked and glowed orange. No one in Meems had ever seen Heaven quite that color before.

Rav pushed on.

He halted to breathe the rain in a flooded plaza that lay before a building with a great, bulging dome. As he rested, panicked Citizens splashed across the empty space, fighting the current to gather with other sky gods in front of the building's high, molded-glass doors. They screamed to be admitted, but the doors did not budge, and Rav quickly lost interest in their fear. He had his own needs. Nothing else mattered to him now.

Another Citizen staggered past. Rav grabbed him.

"Let me go!"

There was a measure of satisfaction in holding this

sky god. But Rav did not indulge in it long. "I will. But
first tell me: Where do the hunter ships bring the sea
folk when the harvest is complete?"

The sky god looked at him wildly, not understanding.

"For the Mother. For the cells! Where do they bring"
—he had to force himself to use the word—"*froggies*
when they harvest them?"

That got through. "Rereceiving hospital . . ." the sky
god stammered. "Follow the avenue . . . to the edge of
the terrace. You'll see the ships there."

Rav pushed the Citizen away and started off. But now
the runoff from the storm was too deep to walk through
with any speed. Rav stopped, pulled off the protective
suit he'd worn since the Xein-craw had saved his life in
the lower desert. Then he arched his back and plunged
into the water.

It was shockingly cold. He tumbled in the strong current, fighting the numbness in his chest when he used his
water lungs. He was strangely frightened, closed in, cut
off from the land and air. You've been with the sky
gods too long! he told himself savagely, quelling the
panic. Water had given him life. He might have learned
to survive in the air, but he would never allow himself to
forget where'd he come from. The sea! Now he swam
with long strokes, righting himself, keeping to the center
of the stream away from flooded vehicles and other
obstacles. And in the water, he chirped again and again
for Luci, praying she'd answer his call.

Then, as he neared the terrace edge, someone chirped
back at him. The voice was frightened, and it came from
a long building off the flooded avenue. As the sky god
had said, hunter ships were berthed there with their
hatches open. Rav could see striplings being pushed
inside the building. Quelling his anger, he climbed out
of the flooded street, onto the mezzanine of the building
nearest the receiving hospital. There he caught his
breath and watched the sky gods finish unloading their
ships. As with the control Unit, security was light: a few
guards armed with the kind of beaming weapons Kip
had taught him to fire down in the Free Zone. He cursed

his lack of foresight in leaving his own weapon behind. That meant he would have to take one.

He took one. The second guard had unfortunately stayed behind to help close a balky hatch cover. He and his partner were too busy trying to get out of the rain to notice Rav popping out of the water behind them. The sea boy snatched the rifle away. Then, when the sky gods recovered from their surprise and went for him, Rav used the weapon as a club. He left them unconscious on the dock.

Rav had seen many strange and terrible things on his way from W'ring, but nothing could have prepared him for what he found inside this building: the huge, shallow pool packed with struggling sea folk; their prayers and frightened cries as they tried to get enough water in their lungs. They cried for the Mother to deliver then, when it was the Mother who had caused their pain. Sickened, he searched the faces, but there was no sign of Luci. Striplings were being taken, a few at a time, through to another chamber. Rav followed the catwalk toward this door—until he found himself face to face with a sky god carrying a rifle just like the one he'd taken.

The sky god's jaw dropped. Then he smiled. "Look at this!" he yelled. "One of the fishies getting smart!"

Other sky gods came out to see what the noise was about. Only the first had a weapon, and he raised it. But one of the his comrades pushed the muzzle aside.

"Don't worry, mate! What harm can he do? He don't know how to shoot that thing, and he'll be fainting from the lack o' water in a minute or two." He stepped forward. "Here's a good frog. Hand it over before you get the Mother angry. Come on, frog—"

Rav shot him. He shot the other two as well, and watched them spin off the catwalk. They floated face down in the pool, and now the noise began to subside. Sea children stared at him. Rav wanted to ignore their questioning faces—hadn't they willingly surrendered to the hunter ships?—but he could not. He gripped the rail.

"Luci of W'ring! Does anyone know her?"

Silence.

"Has anyone seen Luci of W'ring?"

They were from another part of the sea and could not help him. He turned angrily away and went to the next chamber. Here the light was dim; lamps guttered aside the entrance to a white pavilion very much like the Mother's shrine in the sacred grove of the priestess Tahr. A sky god was about to take a stripling inside. Rav stopped her.

"You'll have to wait your turn!" the sky god said indignantly. "And what are you doing with that weapon?"

"Silence! I want a motherling named Luci. From W'ring."

"W'ring? Those fish came through five days ago. What's going on?"

Rav didn't answer. Instead he pushed the curtains aside with the gun muzzle. "What lies inside this tent, woman!"

"They're mindlinked in there. This is the receiving hospital, you know. After your union with the Mother, we bring you out on a gurney, and take you down to your cell. Though with this weather we're having, we won't be loading as many as we ought today."

Rav entered the pavilion. Inside sat a woman dressed in white who held a pair of metal paddles in her hands.

"Welcome," she said. "Please lie down and try to relax. The Mother will be with you very soon."

He shouldered his weapon. "Mother or not, stand aside!"

"What? Guards!"

"Stand aside or die!"

The woman in white dropped the paddles and fled through a side exit as Rav fired again and again into the machine, which was connected by wires to the paddles. Sparks flew, and the lights flickered; dark smoke followed him from the tent. Outside, the Mother's attendant still held onto her stripling, clinging to duty in the face of chaos. Rav ordered the sea child back to the pool.

"You'll never get away with this. The Mother will punish you!"

"If she could punish me, she would have long ago. Now tell me: Do you know where the folk from W'ring were taken?"

"Of course I do."

"Show me. Now!"

"I'm not sure if the loading platform's still in that area."

"Show me!"

Now fear overcame her certainty that no sea boy could possibly behave this way. They went outside, where steaming rain fell in sheets. Rav followed the sky god along a roadway until they reached a gate in the barrier at the terrace edge. She motioned for Rav to come along after she opened it; then lowered a platform by cables until they reached a line of cells in the middle of the complex.

"Twenty-three of them. Starting right here."

Rav wiped water drops from the glass face of the cell nearest him. Inside was a body, lying still, asleep perhaps, or even dead. Rav shuddered as the body twitched. Then he went down the row. He saw striplings and maidens he knew, but none of them was Luci. Groaning with frustration, Rav aimed the weapon again. "Is this all? You're sure!"

"I swear—" But the sky god no longer looked at him. Something had caught her attention overhead. Rav refused to look, fearing a trick. Then he heard a buzzing sound, and something brushed his hair. His head twisted. Janoo! The Xein landed on his shoulder and waved its eye stalk around, chattering rapidly. Rav tried shaking it off.

"Go away! You know I can't understand you!"

The Xein did not let go.

"Leave me, idiot craw! Return to your master and tell him I want no part of his crusade. I'm not fighting anymore. I'm—" And then the platform shook as a beam shot hit it. Rav crouched low and saw sky gods leaning over the rail, aiming their rifles. They had taken

control of the platform as well; slowly the winches
played in the cables. Rav shot back wildly, realized his
attackers had plenty of cover while he had none. Janoo
whistled and took off.

"Go! And tell the Speaker how I met my end!"

But Janoo did not leave. Instead he dove at the
guards, knocking the weapon from the hands of one of
them, scattering the rest. Like an angry bee, he looped
and struck once more; meanwhile the platform reached
the terrace edge again, where Rav could help the Xein.
He was loath to kill again, and did not have to. Between
them, Rav and Janoo got all the rifles. The sea boy
tossed them over the edge with fierce pleasure.

"It seems I was wrong," he said when Janoo landed
on his shoulder again. "I have been fighting all along."
He thought of the frightened sea children in the pool at
the hospital building and had an idea.

"You sky gods! Which of you is capable of piloting
the hunter ships?"

Three of them said they knew how.

"Good. Because you are going to take that 'harvest'
back down to the sea."

"But we can't!" one of the sky gods protested. "The
Mother would never allow it!"

Rav smiled. "Look at me, sky god. Did you ever
imagine the Mother would allow *this*? You'll pilot those
ships, all right. And when we're finished transporting
everyone home again, you have my guarantee of sanc-
tuary—in W'ring."

One by one, then, the sky gods agreed to help.
Perhaps they doubted that Rav really could promise
them safety. But, considering the conditions in the
capital at this moment, perhaps Alissia was not such a
bad idea. With surprising willingness, they went back
into the hospital to begin reloading the ships.

Rowen had taken shelter in the domed Hall of the
Diet of Citizens. When Janoo had not returned, Rowen
had avoided the frightened crowd in front of the great
doors by using a side exit that once had been reserved

for his use alone. The door was unlocked, which was
just as well, since he no longer had keys that fit. This
building was a copy of the hall that stood in Conteirre
City—whose cornerstones, as well as the capping plates
for its dome, had been brought from the homeworld
during the Exodus.

Half horrified, half fascinated, the First Speaker
wandered the empty corridors. Furniture was broken
and scattered about; tapestry hangings depicting
homeworld vistas had faded, their fabric rotting from
neglect. Everything was dirty. Subjectively, it had been
only a few days since Rowen had last seen these hall-
ways, or rather, their original. But now, as his footsteps
raised puffs of dust in the ruined carpets, these forlorn
spaces communicated the disaster that had befallen the
Citizenry more intensely than anything Rowen had ex-
perienced in the canyon since his resurrection.

How could it have happened? How could the
Citizenry ever have allowed itself to be seduced this way
into giving up everything it had worked so hard to
achieve? And where were its representatives now? They
should have been meeting, planning a way to overcome
the present crisis. But everyone had fled: The Diet
Chambers—this hall where Rowen had sought to inspire
his fellow Citizens on so many occasions—was empty.
Was anyone alive now who remembered his words? Or
recalled his power, the great love and respect the
Citizens had for him?

Or maybe you went down in history as a traitor, he
thought. Someone who fled before the greatest battle.

A bleak thought. Rowen wandered the aisles like a
sleepwalker until he reached the foot of the tribune. The
shield of blue and green—the colors of the home-world
—had been replaced by Sinom's starburst, faded almost
to pewter. Rowen put his hand on it, tightened his fist
around a point. When he yanked, more from curiosity
than anger, the starburst crashed to the floor.

The rain drummed on the dome. Rowen turned to
leave.

"Rowen?"

He stopped. Only days had passed since he last heard that voice telling him he was the enemy. That he must be killed. He turned. Mehga, his wife, stood on the tribune, encircled by one of the spotlights. Her loveliness astonished him more, almost, than the fact that she still lived. A faint smile crossed her lips. A tired smile.

"I'm not a ghost, Rowen. Lady Sinom, when she finally got what she wanted, took pains to reward her friends."

"As well as punish her enemies?"

"For a time." The eyes flickered. "Please come closer." Rowen mounted the tribune stairway and stopped when he stood about as far from her as he'd been that day on Weiring terrace.

"You look well, Rowen. It is very pleasant to see you again. More than I deserve."

He whispered a single word: "Why?"

"Does that matter now? After so much time?"

"It was only yesterday."

Mehga sighed. "You must know the answer: visions of immortality. I suppose I must have been wanting to step out from under your shadow. And I was still young, still idealistic, and still afraid. Sinom knew what I was. My weaknesses. Perhaps she brainwashed me. That would make a good excuse—but I did accept her. I wanted what she offered. And I've never cursed the life she gave me. . . . Not like Gaelen does."

"But you betrayed the Citizenry!"

She opened her hands. "The Citizenry, as you can see, still exists. Our population is approximately the same as it was in your day. We're still self-sufficient."

"You"—anguish in his voice—"you betrayed me."

"A political act. Not personal, Rowen."

"We loved each other!"

"Did we? I don't remember. So long ago, dear Speaker. Perhaps we did. Or perhaps, as with Gaelen, our marriage was a convenient one. Better if it was convenience. It makes what happened so much easier to understand. And you less the fool. You were many things before, but never that. Never—"

She closed her eyes suddenly. They were changed when she opened them again.

"They're losing," she said. Rowen remembered Yannika and realized they'd been too optimistic, believing the strike force would go undetected for so long.

"If we fail now, there will certainly be other attempts. We fight until Sinom is overthrown."

But Mehga had not been speaking of the strike force. "Presently there will be nothing to fight for, or with. The Cold is taking them. Her plan has failed. The girl she brought here hasn't strength enough to help." Mehga put her hands on the tribune rail. "If you had been in Gaelen's place, I would have been able to capture her first. Use her against Sinom—she's quite good enough for that. Bring an end to this."

Rowen shook his head. "I don't know who you mean."

"Don't you? The off-worlder? The one that rescued your friend Tyron from the grip of the aborigines."

"Tyron? Alive!" Suddenly what Janoo had been trying to tell him all along made sense. Tyron! The off-worlder who could combine the power of many minds into one, the way the Mother could. Tyron had been trying to contact him, through the Xein.

"Where are they now?"

"At Sinom's house. The Mother's got her, but it isn't working. The Cold is much too strong. So the Mind is doomed. Whether the Cold takes it, or whether your friends succeed in bombing Sinom's house—"

"Killing her will free us!"

"Not now. Not while she and the off-worlder are linked so strongly with the cells in their effort to escape." Mehga laughed, not cruelly, but with some sympathy. "Don't look so shocked, Rowen. Did you really believe your military expedition could accomplish anything? You wanted to free the Citizenry. Your first thought, I'll wager. Free us from one vision of the future in order to enslave us to another. Oh, you practical, rational, powerful man! You should be standing on this tribune now, facing a chamber full of your deputies, with your speech broadcast to every corner of this terrace, and to all the terraces! Hypnotize them with the force of your words, Speaker! Take the podium— here, I give it back to you—and I shall listen with respect while you quell the floods and exorcise the demons from our midst. Open your mouth, Citizen! Save us!''

The whites of her eyes showed as her knees buckled. Rowen caught her in his arms. She felt as she always had: warm, soft, with tensile strenth beneath the softness. She would have to be tried for her crimes. That would be his first duty when the battle was over.

Then the ground began to shake, and water poured through the doors at the lowest tiers of seats beneath the tribune. Rowen touched the transmitter behind his ear and called for Janoo. Perhaps the Xein could reach Yannika in time to halt the attack, at least until she and Rowen could analyze the situation in light of what Mehga had just told him. But he got no response, only static.

Suddenly he realized that fate had limited him. There was only so much of Conteirre he could save now.

Gently, he carried Mehga off the tribune and into the Speaker's Room.

Yannika fused the locks of the control booth doors with a rifle blast. When she went out into the storm, all the floaters were idling, already in formation for the bomb run on Sinom's house. So far, the only casualties were Rowen and the sea boy.

As she took her place in one of the escort craft, she wondered what had happened to them. Rav she could do without—he'd been a grumbler from the start. But Rowen? Rowen would be needed when this was all over. If it were known that he had been along on the fatal raid, that he'd fired a bomb or two himself, he'd be that much more effective when it came to securing the loyalty and cooperation of the Citizens here on Meems, and on the other populated terraces. And there were the sea people to think about too. They'd be the majority, once they were rehabilitated and released from those cells.

"We're ready, Ma," Ruthel said, looking grim. Yannika ruffled his hair. He'd always been fond of that when he was little, and she'd had an impulse to do it one more time, just in case.

"All right!" she yelled. "Let's leave our callin' card, and let's do it right!"

In a swirl of mist and steam, the Free Zone strike force took off, heading west, toward the canyon wall and the circle of green turf.

CHAPTER 28

Tyron waited.

He was not by nature a patient man, but his work for the Citizenry required patience, and so he had disciplined himself to dampen his impulses and gain full value from the strategic pause. And since his resurrection, he had counseled nothing but patience to the offworld girl. However, such advice was easier to give than to follow, and now, with Katya inside the mound and the whole world roaring and shaking, Tyron found his discipline had eroded.

He left Gaelen in the floater and entered the dig. Halfway along the trench, he paused at the place where his cabin had stood. No trace of it remained, though doubtless footings and rotting beams could be located by clearing some of the ground away from the top of the arcade. A fitting monument, he thought. Tyron's relicts.

Sinom's house lay just ahead. The terrace rumbled and shifted, and Tyron knew it was more than the normal movement caused by heavy weather. Something had changed the light; something had affected the weather, too, and that did not bode well for his plans. Katya should have finished with Sinom by now. The

Mind should be dissolving, passing beneath the notice of the mindless protective force he called the Cold. Tyron swallowed, stared at Sinom's door and its stones. Why so nervous? he thought. Can life still be so precious to you, after so long? Perhaps, he thought, I ought to think more like Gaelen.

Of course, if he thought like Gaelen, he would never have considered rescuing a friend who was in difficulty.

Very well, then. He gathered his courage and entered the house of the force that had ruled Conteirre for nearly two thousand years.

Inside it was dark, and it took him a moment to adjust to what light there was. When he did, the breath caught in his throat. Two bodies lay on the bed. One of them, dressed in a white gown that was wet now in the middle, was the old woman; and she had Katya's head locked in her deadly soft embrace.

At first, Tyron feared they were both dead. Then they both shuddered, bodies linked in horrible synchronization. Everything together: the breathing, the slow, faint heartbeat, the pulses of their linked minds. Sinom's wheelchair had overturned, and both had fallen together on the bed. Tyron cursed. The girl had ignored his warning and failed to touch the stones that would have protected her. The floor shook again. Something had to be done. Then Tyron realized that the aboriginal minds could still be contacted through the stones. Perhaps, if Katya touched them now, with his help, she could escape the terrible embrace that was killing her, and what was left of Conteirre.

Hesitantly Tyron touched Katya's shoulder. It was as cold as ice, and she did not respond. Simon didn't either, but when he tried prying them apart, he failed. Their struggle had welded them together. If he wanted Katya to come into contact with the stones, he had no choice but to drag both of them across the room.

He pulled. When their bodies fell from the bed, Tyron winced, fearing the fall would shatter them like pots. They were heavier than seemed possible for two small people; it was as though Tyron were pulling the weight of the Mind—and the Cold—as well. His heart pounded, and sweat salted his eyes, but he moved them. Four feet away now . . . three . . . His feet slipped on the stone floor—his good fortune. For Gaelen had struck at him from behind. The blow missed, leaving the Speaker off-balance. Tyron scrambled up, putting his shoulder into Gaelen's stomach, driving him past the stones and out into the trench, until they were rolling, each trying for the one strike that would silence the other.

"Don't . . . know what you're doing!" Tyron gasped. Gaelen's answer produced an explosion of pain as he brought a loose rock hard onto the back of the old man's head. His will was strong, but the exertion and shock were too much. He lost his hold on Gaelen, lost sight of him as consciousness faded. When it returned a moment later, Gaelen stood over him, aiming a hand pistol. Something like pleasure—a replica of pleasure— filled the speaker. He was about to take a life with his own hands! Nearness to death sparked within the cold soul, and his fingers trembled on the trigger.

Tyron opened his mouth to plead, not for his own life, but for that of his world. He never got the chance. Roaring filled his ears; shattering impact tossed him back like a bit of stuffed cloth almost to the end of the arcade. Wetness on his face—blood? I'm finally dying, he thought with a certain satisfaction. But he could not help feeling his face with his hands, and when he looked at them, he discovered the wetness was only water and chips of ice. He staggered up, ears ringing, and looked for Gaelen.

He found him, dead—skewered by a fifteen-foot shaft of ice that had broken free from the next terrace up. Part of the icicle had shattered into ice chunks that now completely covered the entrance to Sinom's house. Tyron stared at it a moment. Perhaps there might have been a way to reason with Gaelen. But there was no way to reason with the ice.

He ran to the pile and began digging through it with both hands.

* * *

The hospital on Oran was small—just four mud-plaster buildings each shaded by a huge plane tree. But it had a maternity room, and Katya who was barely fourteen years old then, had been fascinated by it. For her, as for any young girl, the mechanics of childbirth were a rather sinister mystery surrounding a single idea: pain. So when a woman in labor finally was brought into the room, Katya had hidden in some bushes just outside and, very gently, touched the mind of the mother-to-be. She'd not been prepared for the shock, and quickly broke off the contact, more out of consideration for the hardworking woman than from fear of the actual pain itself.

What she was experiencing now, trying to hold onto the Mind, was close to what she'd felt on Oran. But now she was at the very end of her endurance; and she knew that this "child"—the Mind Simon had given life to and nurtured—was never to be born.

The Cold had taken it. Vast, without intention or morality, performing the only task it existed for, this relentless current across the bounds of time and space was gradually consuming the Mind of Conteirre. Much as Katya feared it, there was something admirable about such cold-blooded efficiency. And she could detect a peace of sorts deep within this prison. Perhaps, also, the company of other Minds that had resigned themselves to their fate.

As Sinom would not. She squeezed the life from every cell to gain more energy, and would lash out at Katya for refusing to be so cruel. Indeed, Katya had tried to dampen the struggle. She did her best, as much as Sinom would allow, to comfort the thousands of frightened souls under her control. If it were possible, she'd release them at once. But then the Cold would take Sinom utterly away. And Sinom still had Katya. All Katya could do, then, was try to hold her ground, keep her identity against all the lives that were in her hands.

And Sinom's life. Fate had punished the old woman, rendered judgment on her ambition to become something more than Creation had intended. We must sense those limits, and must never attempt to smash them. That was the lesson the Mother had never learned, she and her Mind; and because she had not accepted her place, she must be separated from the parts of Creation that had. That was the Cold's purpose. Unjust, but necessary.

But what of *my* life? Katya thought. I had no ambition. I just wanted a home, and the same chance for happiness any woman might have. I wanted my brother to be happy too. Twins . . . They were wrong to tell us that. We're really one thing that was split in two: Jes with the ambition, I with the power. We moaned about it, but that was the thing that saved both our lives, until Sinom found us and forced us together by tearing us apart. Perhaps it's just as well.

Fight, girl! Fight! She felt very cold. Calm, too. She had not risked what Sinom had, and the loss for Katya was that much less. Only two lives. The worlds will live and die without us. They were sinking deeper into the Cold with every moment. And in the thousands of cells along the Meems terrace and elsewhere, the bodies strained with the effort to resist. Thousands of hearts racing. Thousands of individual terrors combined.

In her own body, Sinom moaned. Her control slipped. She lost her hold on something that was vital to her plans. Something she had surrounded, the way an amoeba surrounds a drop of food, but not absorbed, because another Mind had got it first.

Katty?

That voice! Katya's thoughts were dull. She recognized something of that voice, but it was fearsome and sad, a voice of ancient power.

Katty! Hold on. I can reach you.

No. Another trick of Sinom's. Her brother was certainly lost, deep in the Mind, deep in the Cold. But why was the Mother shrieking, and where did the force that pried her away from her embrace come from? A sensation of rushing headlong through a dark tunnel—speed with no reference—made her giddy.

She felt cold stone underneath her. The Mother lay a little way off, moaning softly.

"Come on, Sis, you've gotta get up!" She was yanked to her feet.

"The Mind . . . still linked—"

"Oh, Christ." Jes put his arm around her waist, took one look at the blocked doorway, lowered his head, *pushed . . .*

The ice scattered. Tyron, who'd been working to clear the rubble, suddenly found himself looking at the twins.

"Is she . . ."

"Old man, I don't know who you are, but if you don't get the hell out of here you're gonna be chopped meat. Look what's coming at us!"

Tyron turned. From the lower part of the terrace flew a squad of screaming floaters headed straight for the mound. Tyron grabbed Katya's other arm, and together they pulled her away fom Sinom's house.

Get down! A voice sounded inside his head, forcing him to the grass as the first bombs hit the mound. Concussions pushed them toward the edge of the chasm; the floaters wheeled in tight formation, made another pass, dropped more bombs. Flames spouted from the mound, turning it into a miniature caldera. They came back one more time, and when they were through, Sinom's home was gone. And with it, the temple of the aborigines.

Something like a sigh whispered through the canyon.

Katty? You still got it?

Yes. The Cold's taken her . . . and the other Mind.

It'll be back. You've got to let the cells go. But we've got one more thing to do first.

Too . . . weak.

I'll help you. Come on. Just one more thing.

Tyron watched Jesse hug his sister. His own eyes blurred—the off-worlders seemed to merge—and they rose away from their bodies and out above the edge of the canyon, where the mirrors reflected fierce sunlight onto the boiling vault of ice.

We gotta move 'em, Kat.

Don't know . . . how.

Use the Mind! I'll lead you.
You?
Yeah, me.

He showed her. They entered the hydraulics, turned valves, forced the cradles to turn. Slowly the mirrors backed away from the sun until they rested on the sand once again. Jes helped Katya to the terrace. Together they forced the boiling water to cool. Then, with Katya at the point of exhaustion, they released the groupmind of Conteirre.

Inside the cells, one by one, Citizens began to wake up.

Mehga shuddered and opened her eyes.

"She's gone."

"Please lie still, Mehga."

"No. Take me outside. We must go—you must go—where our people are."

The illusion of her youth was vanishing before his eyes. Rowen feared she might crumble to dust; and so he helped her. Together they walked through the flooded Diet Hall, past the rotunda, to open the great doors that Gaelen had ordered locked. There the frantic crowd pressed forward. The people in it were soaked, and they huddled close enough together to make steam. The First Speaker looked out at them, unable to frame his thoughts. How could he comfort them? What could he possibly tell them that would make them accept the destruction that certainly awaited what was left of the Citizenry? He knew no such words, for defeat was alien to him. And yet—

The rain stopped. Rowen looked up and saw that the light had changed again. *She's gone.* Could it be true? They were looking at him now, waiting. He opened his arms to them.

"Citizens of Conteirre!" he began. It was as if he had never left at all.

CHAPTER 29

Tyron, Katya, and Jesse sat in the salon of Dink Morgan's limousine. The twins drank soup; Tyron, nursing a two-thousand-year thirst and a declining case of nerves, was sipping a glass of Morgan's Armagnac. Off-worlder stuff though it was, Tyron pronounced it fit to drink. He spoke the language of Conteirre; and neither twin had trouble understanding him.

"Now," Tyron said, after a loud sigh, "maybe you'll tell me how you freed yourselves."

Jes smiles. "Go ahead, sis. Tell him."

"I'm not quite sure myself," she said, returning the smile. "Sinom gave me control of most of the Mind. I was to hold onto it while she tried to break contact with the Cold. She was using herself as a kind of shield, and it wasn't working. The Cold was just too strong. I got the feeling that it had become impatient after so many years. I think Sinom had resisted far longer than anyone else ever had. Anyway, we were losing. I remember thinking that maybe it wouldn't be so bad on the other side of the Cold, wherever that might be. The company of other great Minds—"

"Most quite insane," Tyron pointed out.

"Yes. I suppose they would be. Anyway, I might have been able to escape if I had just let go of the Mind, but I couldn't. They were all so frightened! I was trying to do my best to comfort everybody, telling them I'd stay with them no matter what. We were all going down, and then . . ." She shook her head.

"Don't give *me* any credit, Kat! Jeez." Jes stood up. "Why can't you admit that for once *I* got you out of a jam? It took me a while to realize I could move around, do things. I sensed Katty in trouble and I tried to protect her. Like hugging someone. That's what it felt like. And I guess the old lady was so busy trying to get away from the Cold, and hanging onto Katty by a few threads, that she couldn't do anything about me. The Cold sucked her in, I hung onto Kat, she kept the Mind. We stopped the rain—*we* stopped it—then let go before the Cold could get a grip on us again."

Tyron grunted. "So it seems. Yet how were you able to do all that? Your sister told me that you had no mental capabilities of that sort."

"But I touched the stones! Just for a second, before Sinom grabbed me, but it was enough. I made contact with that other Mind—the people who lived here before you. I heard their voices." Jes looked pale, and Tyron nodded.

"I felt them too."

"Then you know that they could keep Sinom from linking with me. And they did something else, too. Power, like Kat's. Maybe I always had it, but couldn't see how to use it. I was so busy feeling sorry for myself. Never stopped long enough to hear the silence. Reach in. I don't know. Anyway, they helped me. I think they wanted Kat, and me, and all those people Sinom controlled to escape. Then they took Sinom. What they wanted all along."

"Why?" Katya asked. "So she could be punished?"

"That's what the old woman thought, but I don't think that. I think they need her. They needed all the Minds they've gathered in the Cold. And Sinom's, too.

Maybe they intend to go on. Make a place for themselves where their kind won't harm things like us."

"Another universe. They were created. Now they become creators themselves. The cycle goes on."

"The snake devouring its own tail," Tyron said softly.

"Something like that." Jes had been rummaging through the pantry. Suddenly he pulled out a glass jar. "Say, I'm starved! Who's for some caviar sandwiches?"

Rowen had no hesitation about occupying the Speaker's offices. With Megha at his side lending authority, he soon had what staff remained in the Diet Hall engaged in cleaning it up. Communication with both the political and technical administrators had begun, and Rowen had discovered that most of these key Citizens, though cowed by the long period of darkness that had covered the world, were nevertheless capable and willing to assist in the business of rebuilding the world. There were still serious problems—notably with the life-support systems, which suffered from neglected maintenance. But there was also the excitement of beginning again. Rowen had not felt that excitement for a long time.

And he would have Yannika's help. The chief Mechanic of the Free Zone had burst into his office shortly after he himself had taken it over to report the success of the bombing mission.

"She's nothin' but dust now, Speaker! Nothing left alive."

"Nothing . . ." Rowen remembered Tyron then. Losing his old friend would have been bad enough in the old days. But to have lost him now, after so much had happened, when he needed him more than he ever had, showed how cruel fate could be.

"Well, nothin' to speak of. We did spot an off-world ship, though, not too far away. Sent Kippy and Ruthel down for a look and we found these three havin' a picnic, easy as you please. One of em's an old crow claims he's a personal friend of yours! Kippy!''

The door opened. Tyron stomped in, looking a little battered, fierce as ever in a purple fur coat that was several sizes too big for him. The Speaker rose.

''Tyron!''

The Archaeologist yanked his arm away from Yannika's boy. ''So there you are! Cowering in your office, as I might have expected. Afraid of a little rain, are you?''

Rowen could think of nothing to say. Instead, laughing, crying, he embraced the old man, until Tyron shoved him off.

''And where's that worthless hubcap of yours? It was supposed to tell you I was out''

''Janoo tried. But it was damaged, and lost part of its memory.'' Rowen looked quizzical. ''Have you seen Janoo, Yannika?''

''Not since you two went after the fish boy. You never found him, did you?''

''No . . . Tyron, my transmitter's not working. Can you call Janoo?''

''Oh, all right!'' Tyron touched the skin behind his ears. After a moment, he scowled.

''Well?''

''Made contact all right. But Janoo won't be back for a while.''

''Why not?''

''It said it's too busy!''

The priestess Tahr rose to the surface, near the place where her acolytes had seen the body fall. Choppy waves and heavy rain made it difficult to find at first, but then Tahr saw the shiny heads of the sea folk who had gathered to see what had come down from Heaven.

Tahr chirped impatiently; the crowd parted. Then, floating face down in the water, was the body of a sea child. Her acolytes had told her the impact had been fearsome. Gently, Tahr felt for a neck pulse, and found that a faint one still beat there. She turned the body over.

It was Luci of W'ring.

"What does it mean, priestess?"

"Has she come from Heaven?"

"Why has the Mother sent her back? Tell us, priestess, tell us, please!"

"Silence!" To her acolytes: "Take this child to my home. We must save her if we can." Then to the crowd: "If this be a sign, I must consider its meaning. Return to your homes. I will summon you again when the Mother has revealed her will to me."

There was a disappointed murmur, and some of the bobbing heads sank beneath the surface. But then a familiar rumble trembled through the waters, and the old fear seized all their hearts, even that of the priestess.

Out of the rain came the fleet of hunter ships. The ships stopped their engines, put out their anchors. Their quarry watched in horror, not able to flee in that moment of shock. The hatches opened.

Sea children emerged, leaping joyously into their home.

The twins sat in the couches on the flight deck of their ship, warming the inductors for the boost out of the canyon and into orbit. They had plenty of power now, enough to return to populated worlds with the message Rowen has asked them to carry. The days of secrecy and isolation were over. The Citizenry needed help, and trade, and contact with other worlds and peoples. Jesse and Katya had agreed to act as roving ambassadors. For the first time in their lives they had a purpose.

Slowly the limousine lifted off Meems terrace, up through the slot that had melted through the remains of the ice vault. Clouds and bridges and bands of pink sand and green farmland shrank away until they were bare lines in a narrow aperture on an otherwise lifeless planet. Jes let Katya program the navigator for the jump into chord as he stared at the screens.

Jes?

The thought came back to her. Under Jes's own power now. *Yeah, sis?*

Only one thing still bothers me. You saw her face, didn't you?

Yup.

What was it like?

Wanna see?

No—no, I don't think so. I'd rather you just told me.

Jesse grinned. "Let me put it this way, Katty," he said. "Put a few years on you, and you might've passed for sisters."

Then he hit the lever, and the ship stretched across the arc of space.